"Guess that old saying is true. Everything looks different in the light of day."

Shelby turned to fix her gaze on the tall figure at her side holding the baby carrier easily against his chest. That sight *was* different.

"I'm going to look around and see what I can find." Jax settled the baby carrier down on the wooden slats at her feet.

Clearly he expected her to stay put and watch over the foundling. Clearly the man did not understand that Shelby Grace was finished doing what other people expected. It took her only a moment to bend and unsnap the safety latches. She lifted the baby and cuddled her close, even as she headed to the steps to follow Jax.

"No one in Sunnyside would have been able to hide a pregnancy, much less a baby for three months."

"You honestly think there are no secrets in this town?" He looked back over his shoulder at her. "Would you say everybody here knows all there is to know about you, Shelby Grace?"

ANNIE JONES

Winner of a Holt Medallion for Southern-themed fiction, and the *Houston Chronicle*'s Best Christian Fiction Author of 1999, Annie Jones grew up in a family that loved to laugh, eat and talk—often all at the same time. They instilled in her the gift of sharing through words and humor, and the confidence to go after her heart's desire (and to act fast if she wanted the last chicken leg). A former social worker, she feels called to be a "voice for the voiceless" and has carried that calling into her writing by creating characters often overlooked in our fast-paced culture—from seventysomethings who still have a zest for life to women over thirty with big mouths and hearts to match. Having moved thirteen times during her marriage, she is currently living in rural Kentucky with her husband and two children.

Bundle of Joy

Annie Jones

HARLEQUIN® LOVE INSPIRED®

Recycling programs for this product may not exist in your area.

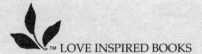

™ LOVE INSPIRED BOOKS

ISBN-13: 978-0-373-87801-7

BUNDLE OF JOY

www.LoveInspiredBooks.com

Printed in U.S.A.

People were also bringing babies to Jesus
to have him touch them. When the disciples
saw this, they rebuked them. But Jesus called the
children to him and said, "Let the little children
come to me, and do not hinder them, for the
kingdom of God belongs to such as these."
—*Luke* 18:15–16

For my family, who give me the peace
when I need to write and plenty of space
if I can't get any writing done.

Chapter One

Nobody did anything without a reason, though reason was rarely behind the things that people did. Jackson Stroud didn't just believe that; he counted on it.

Guilt. Anger. Pain. Longing. The motivations were often so deep-seated that they were difficult to name. But Jackson—Jax, to people who thought they knew him well—knew what made people tick, or at least he figured it out more quickly than the average Joe.

That knack had served him well these past four years on the Dallas police force. Not as well in his so-called "personal life." Despite the best efforts of the older ladies at his church to set him up with perfectly lovely women, he'd never been able to turn off the drive to figure people out long enough to make a real connection. Certainly not long enough to settle down. He'd accepted ages ago that he was not the settling-down type.

"Okay by me," he muttered to himself in the darkness of his truck cab. That just meant there were no broken hearts in his wake when he moved on. Jackson Stroud always moved on.

So when he veered off the brightly lit highway down a darkened ramp in the middle of the night, he did not do so lightly. Bone tired, he needed to stretch his legs, get some coffee and maybe…

From nowhere, the headlights of a silver SUV speeding precariously close to the centerline slashed across Jax's line of vision. He hit the brakes and swerved toward the shoulder. His own lights came to rest on a dark sign by the road: Y'all Come Back to Sunnyside, Texas.

He grumbled under his breath, then guided his truck back onto the road and drove on until he pulled into the well-lit parking lot, under the signs Delta's Shoppers' Emporium and Truck Stop Inn and The Crosspoint Café. Framed by huge glass windows, a lone clerk stood at a counter. He was intently texting at his post.

Jax's boots hit the ground with a thud. He rubbed his eyes, then his jaw. He needed a shave. He knew he looked rough—but felt only hungry.

He put his hand over his stomach, but it was his conscience that made him admit that hunger had not led him to take the off-ramp tonight. Somewhere in the darkness of this warm spring night, it had dawned on him that without the familiar trappings of his work around him, he suddenly felt cast adrift.

He turned toward the Crosspoint Café. A hot meal, maybe a conversation with a waitress who would call him "honey" and make him feel, at least for a few minutes, like he wasn't all alone in the big, wide world— that was all he needed. He reached into his truck to grab his steel-gray Stetson, slammed the door shut, then took a step in that direction. The lights inside went out.

"Hey, if you want something, you'd better hurry." The clerk stood in the mini-mart's open door a few yards away. He shouted, "Whole place shuts down in twenty minutes!"

"Café already looks closed." Jax gave a nod and started toward the mini-mart.

"Yeah?" The lanky young clerk frowned, then shrugged it off. "Maybe Miz Shelby has something to do."

"Miz Shelby?" Jax chuckled softly, instantly picturing a sassy red-haired Southern belle in a pink waitress uniform and white apron, smacking gum and pouring out advice about life as freely as she did rich black coffee while she flirted with her transient clientele. "Maybe Miz Shelby met a handsome stranger and—"

"Hey! Don't you say stuff like that about Miz Shelby! She taught Sunday school to almost every kid in Sunnyside at some time or another, and for your information, she don't even know any strangers."

Jax fought the urge to argue that not knowing someone was what made them a stranger. "Sorry, kid. I didn't mean anything by it. I'm sure Miz Shelby is a fine lady."

In his imagination, the unseen Miz Shelby's hair was now white, her face lined and her life full but still missing something.

"You bet she is. Even if she wasn't, ain't been no one around to run off with, anyways." The young man with the name tag reading Tyler on his blue-and-white-striped shirt leaned back against the open door and checked his phone again. "You showing up and a jerk who tried to steal some gas are the only action I've seen around all night."

Not that the kid could see much of anything beyond the small screen in his hand, Jax thought. Then his mind went to the speeding SUV. Like any good cop, he wondered if there was a connection, if something more was going on.

Before he could ask the kid about the incident, the sound of a cat mewing caught his attention. Maybe not a mew—definitely the cry of a small animal, though, probably rooting for food out there in the lonely night.

"Anyways," the kid said, heading back inside, "I don't know what's up with Miz Shelby, but I'm locking the doors at eleven."

Jax nodded. No gas stolen. Not his jurisdiction—or his business. He decided to let it go and followed the kid inside.

The sound demanded his attention again. Close to the café, maybe on the wide, rough-hewn wooden deck? Jax turned to pinpoint it and caught a movement briefly blocking the dim light from inside the café. Someone was moving around inside.

A screech of a wooden table leg on concrete. The clank of metal, followed by a crash of dishes. A shuffling sound. Then a soft whimper of that small animal in the darkness. Was something up in the café, which had closed uncharacteristically early? Was there an injured animal nearby that needed help?

The sound was none of his business, either, but he wouldn't be able to walk away not knowing if there was something he should have done and didn't. The boards of the café steps creaked under Jax's boots. He wished he had a flashlight. A shape filled the glass window in the café door. He started to call out for whoever had closed the café to stay put until he could check things out, but the subtle mewing drew his attention again.

He glanced down to find a square plastic laundry basket covered with small blue-and-white blankets. Something moved slightly without revealing anything beneath the blankets. He thought of the sound and drew a quick conclusion. Someone, probably knowing good ol' lonely, grandmotherly type Miz Shelby worked the late shift at the Crosspoint, had left a basket of kittens on the doorstep.

The doorknob of the café rattled, and Jax bent down to snag the basket. "Hold it, there's a—"

The sickening *thwock* of the door whacking his head rang out in the night. The door had knocked his hat clean off, but thanks to a gentle nudge from him, the basket had been spared.

"Ow." He squeezed his eyes shut for a split second. When he straightened up and opened them again, he found himself gazing into the biggest, bluest, most startled eyes he'd ever seen. Eyes that were wet with tears.

"What hap... Why...?" The young woman staggered back a step, clutching a folded piece of paper and an overstuffed backpack covered with multicolored embroidered flowers.

She was just a little bit of a thing. The brief glimpse of her outline through the window had told him that much. It hadn't told him that she was maybe in her late twenties. Or that when he looked into her face, his heart would race, just a little.

"Don't tell me. *You're* Miz—"

"I'm sorry...I was just... We're closed." Still standing in the threshold, with the main door open slightly behind her and the screen door open just a sliver in front of her, she set the colorfully decorated backpack down. She glanced around behind her, then set her jaw and reached inside to flip on an outside light. "I know the sign says our hours go later, but tonight we're closed. Goodbye."

Her tone had started out steady, had faded and then had ended firmly again.

He bent slowly to snatch up his hat. His banged-up temple began to throb. "I could see that you were closed. That's why I came over here."

"You came here *because* you saw that we were closed?" She stiffened, then leaned out enough to steal a peek outside, her gaze lingering on the lights of the store, where Tyler was texting away, paying them no notice.

That afforded Jax a moment to take in the sight of her. And what a sight. Her hair was neither blond nor brown, with streaks that beauticians might work hours to try to produce but only time in the sun could create.

When she caught him studying her, she blushed from the quivering tip of her chin to the freckled bridge of her nose. Her lips trembled. He thought for a moment she'd burst out crying, as the telltale tears proved she had been doing. She was obviously in a highly emotional state. Scared, maybe. Vulnerable, definitely.

He put one hand out to try to soothe her. He wasn't sure what he would say, but he would speak in a soft, re-assuring tone. He'd help her because…well, that's what Jax did. He helped. Whenever and wherever he could. "It's all right. I just—"

"Didn't you hear me? We're closed, cowboy." Her posture relayed a confidence her voice did not. "Go."

She blinked a few times, fast, but tears did not well up in her eyes. In fact, Jax got the feeling that if she could have made it happen, fire would have shot from them. And that fire would singe his hide considerably.

That thought made him grin. "Actually, I'm not a cowboy so much as I'm here to—"

"I don't care who you are or what you want. You need to leave here and be whoever you are elsewhere." She gripped the edge of the door as if it were the rail-ing on a sinking ship.

The sight of her small hand white-knuckled against the rough wood stirred something protective in his gut, even as her insistence that he leave tweaked his suspi-cions about what was going on here. Was there a mes-sage in her behavior? Was his instant attraction to the lady throwing off his finely honed ability to sense dan-ger and motivation?

"I'm Jax." The name that no one had called him for so long came out quickly and naturally in her presence. "That is, *you* can call me Jax."

"Jax?" Her lips formed the name slowly. She shook her head, as if she didn't understand why he was still standing there, whatever he asked to be called.

"That is, I'm Jackson Stroud." He steadied the small

basket at his feet, then stood tall, settled his hat on his head, lowered his chin slightly and added with what he hoped was a disarming smile, "Kitten rescuer."

"Kitten...?" She glanced downward at the basket, which she might have knocked over with the door if she hadn't beaned Jax instead. Yet she didn't seem the least bit concerned about the injury to his head.

The screen door creaked loudly as she came outside at last. She knelt down, peeked under the blankets, then turned her face to look at him. The fire in her now had an ominous quality, as if the first sparks of suspicion had become a bed of banked embers that had the potential to smolder on for a very long time. "What is the matter with you?"

"Well, I did recently take a rather nasty blow to the head." He rubbed his temple and gave her a grin.

The clerk stuck his head out the door again. "Everything okay over there, Shelby Grace?"

"Shelby Grace," Jax murmured. He liked that better than Miz Shelby. It felt good to say, all Southern charm with a touch of faith. She sounded like a woman he could reason with, maybe even win over if she'd just listen and—

"Call Sheriff Denby, Tyler." She bent over the basket and fussed with the blankets for a moment.

"He ain't gonna like being woke up this time of night," the thin young man called back.

"Sheriff? There's no call for that." Jax took a step back as he dipped his hand into his pocket to withdraw his badge. Wait. He didn't have it on him anymore, and even if he did, it wouldn't mean anything here and now.

He stepped back again and held his hands up. "I was just trying to do the right thing, ma'am."

"The right thing? You have the gall to talk to me about…" She gathered the blankets back up again, reached into the basket, lifted the contents out all at once and stood. "Call Denby, Tyler. Tell him it's an emergency. We have a no-account lowlife here who just tried to abandon a baby on my doorstep!"

Chapter Two

"Baby!" The ruggedly handsome cowboy standing inches away from the doorway of the Crosspoint Café looked genuinely shocked at that news. "Lady, I don't have a baby, but if I did, nothing in the world would make me drop it off somewhere and walk away."

She wanted to believe him. But then, Shelby tended to want to believe everyone—her dreamer of a dad, her liar of an ex-boyfriend, all her friends and coworkers who told her that things weren't as bad as they seemed. And she had paid the price for that.

Shelby drew in a deep breath and went over the three promises she had made to herself last night. She had felt so strongly about them, she had included them in the note still clutched in her hand.

1. Never forget that with God all things are possible.

2. Never let anyone else tell her what she "should" feel.

3. *Never, ever* trust a cowboy.

"I'd like to say I believe you, but…"

She skimmed her gaze over the man before her. Tall, lean, dark-haired, with steely eyes burning into her from the shadow of a gray Stetson. He was the picture of cool, calm and all-cowboy. The culmination of years of disappointment in men like this made it impossible for her to simply trust whatever this one had to say.

"But I did come out and find you bent over this basket. How do I know you didn't leave it and weren't just about to take off?"

"Sheriff Denby says to stay put. He'll get here as soon as he can," called Tyler Sprague, the teenage clerk, whom Shelby had known since she'd watched him in the church nursery.

"Okay." Shelby clutched the basket close, relieved to have a chance to look away from the stranger. "Let's get her inside."

The cowboy cocked his head. *"Her?"*

She stopped mid-turn, her foot raised above the threshold. "What?"

He leaned in close. Closer than she'd normally have allowed a man to get to her, especially one she didn't know. "You called the baby her."

She could hear her own heart beating. Heat surged up from her neck to her cheeks, then all the way to the tops of her ears. She raised her chin to try to look beyond the man who had just challenged her—in more ways than one—to the kid standing behind him. "We're taking *him or her* inside, Tyler."

The young man gave the thumbs-up even as he began heading for the mini-mart entrance. "I'll close up and come over."

The man held the door open for her and the baby in the basket, waiting until she passed so close that the blankets brushed against the sleeve of his denim jacket. Then he murmured, "You said *her*."

Shelby went sailing across the threshold, which she thought she would never cross again, her head held high. "I didn't want to say *it*. Babies are human beings, not its."

Once inside, he whisked his hat off his head like a true Texas gentleman. "That much I agree with, but still…"

"Just what are you accusing me of?" She set the basket down on the tabletop. She could see the man's eyes much better now. That wasn't making it any easier for her to talk to him. She bent her head and gazed down at the infant's small, sweet face instead. "That is what you're doing, right? Accusing me of something?"

"I was just asking a question." He stood there for a moment, with expectation hanging in the air between them.

Shelby had never been grilled by the police in her life, but she kind of got the feeling this was how it would be. She pressed her lips closed, getting the sense that anything she said could and would be used against her. And yet she didn't feel threatened so much as…

His gaze sank into hers.

She took a quick, sharp breath and didn't let it out until he looked into the basket. His eyes narrowed. After a moment, he shook his head. "What kind of person would not only forsake their child, but also leave it alone in the night outside a closed café?"

"We weren't supposed to be closed," Shelby said softly, unable to take her eyes off the small pink child in the basket. A baby whose appearance here tonight had foiled her big plans.

The baby stretched and squirmed. Long lashes stirred, then lifted. The baby looked right at Shelby, then at the road-weary, bleary-eyed cowboy.

"She's so… I just don't see how anyone could…" The word strangled in Shelby's throat. Tears burned in her eyes—again. She would have thought after the past few days, since she had made up her mind what she had to do, that she'd cried all the tears she'd been allotted for a lifetime. But nope, here they were again. "I'm sorry. It's just been a long day and…"

"Her eyes are blue," he murmured.

"Lots of babies have blue eyes at first," she assured him, swiping away what she resolved would be her last tear with the back of her hand.

"*Your* eyes are blue." He jerked his head up to nail her with a discerning stare.

Really? This total stranger, this cowboy kitten rescuer, was testing her like that? Any other time in her life, she would have stumbled all over herself to assure him she was above reproach…because, well, she was in this instance. But tonight, with her new resolve to take charge of her life, she decided to give as good as she got.

She gave one last sniffle, then moved around the suspicious, questioning cowboy slowly, her gaze fixed on his face. "You just called the baby *her*."

He glowered at her—for about two seconds. His smile broke over his face slowly, not at all like the bold grin he had flashed at her earlier that had thrown her completely off-kilter. This smile, and the way his broad shoulders relaxed as he rubbed the back of his neck and shook his head as a concession to her standing up to him, warmed Shelby to the very pit of her clenched stomach.

"Maybe we should look for a note or something." He started to reach into the tangle of flannel blankets.

"Wait." She stuck her hand out to stop him. The instant her fingertips brushed his jacket, her breath went still. She curled her fist against her chest and managed to sound a little less flustered than she felt as she asked, "Won't the police want to look for fingerprints?"

"Not likely. First of all, you won't get prints off flannel. Besides that, unless whoever left this baby has a criminal record in a database easily accessed by the local cops, it really won't be an issue." He reached in, cradled the whole body of the small infant in his large, strong hands, then lifted the baby up.

Despite her clashing emotions, Shelby couldn't keep herself from smiling at the sight of the cowboy and child framed by the window of the silent café. "You seem pretty sure of what you're doing."

"Spent a lot of time in foster care. I learned a lot about looking after little ones." He shifted to get the baby situated right against his broad shoulder.

"No, I meant..."

The baby let out a soft sound, then snuggled in close, drawing its legs up. A tiny milk bubble formed on the sweet little lips, which made those chubby pink cheeks almost unbearably pinchable.

The stranger leaned back to check out what was going on with the baby. Then he smiled—just a little and only for a half a second at most.

Shelby sighed.

"Around here, everybody knows how to tend to babies and children and old folks and…whatever needs tending to." Except the one guy she had hitched her heart to, she couldn't help noting to herself. Mitch Warner hadn't known how to take care of anyone but himself, and he'd even done that poorly. "What I meant was that you seem to know a lot about police work."

"*That* I picked up *after* foster care." He began to pat the child's back.

She stood there, probably looking like a deer in the headlights, waiting for him to elaborate. How did he pick up his knowledge of police procedures? Was he the type to associate with lawmen…or lawbreakers?

"Why don't you check for a note?" He jiggled the baby slightly and nodded toward the basket.

She rifled through the tangle of pastel-colored flannel blankets. "Here are a few disposable diapers and a full bottle. Nothing else. No note. No personal items."

"I figured as much."

She looked up to find him staring at her. Or, more accurately, straight into her—as though he were searching for something she wanted to keep covered up.

He settled the still sleeping child back into the basket. Shelby reached out to pull the top blanket up over the baby. He did the same.

Their hands brushed. The warmth of his callused palm eased through her chilled fingers.

This time she did not yank away, but let her hand flit from the blanket to the baby's soft curls and on to its soft, plump cheek. "If you don't mind, I was just going to tuck the baby in and say a little prayer for… the baby…and for whoever left the baby here."

He nodded. "That's kind of you. I'm more than a little ashamed that I didn't think to offer that myself."

That caught her off guard. "You want to join me in a prayer?"

"For the child, yes, ma'am, I would. I don't know if I can be so gracious toward the one who walked off and left her…." He bowed his head and shut his eyes, then opened them once again to nail Shelby with a look as he added, "Or him."

Shelby took a deep breath, acknowledged both the remark and the reservations they both still held for one another with a curt nod. "All right, then…"

"Jackson Stroud." He held his hand out.

"Shelby Grace Lockhart." She gave his hand a quick, firm shake and, just before she let her hand slip from his, added in a soft whisper, "Jax."

The use of the name he had first given her seemed to hit home with him. It appeared to set him off his game for a split second before he nodded to her and bowed his head.

She bowed her head, too, but she did not close her eyes. Instead she focused her gaze on the compelling face of this innocent, seemingly unwanted child as she prayed.

"Every creature matters to you, Lord. Everyone is loved. Sometimes it's hard to remember that none of us is ever truly alone when we feel lost. Sometimes it's hard to know what to do and who to trust. Please, Lord, help me…help us…to show your love to this newcomer. And through it all, let us not forget your mercy for whoever found themselves in a place where they thought it best to leave this precious one here tonight. We place them and ourselves in your loving hands. Amen."

"Amen," he murmured.

"Amen? Y'all holding a revival in here or something?" Tyler came striding in with his phone in one hand and earbuds swinging in his other with every step. "The store is all locked up tight. Sheriff Denby just pulled up outside."

Shelby spun around to face Tyler, her heart pounding. A mix of panic and embarrassment swirled through her at the idea of being seen praying with this man, whom she had met only moments ago and clearly had no reason to fully trust.

"Just another hard luck case for Shelby Grace," she could imagine folks saying. Someone else who would fill her head with promises and her heart with hope, when anyone else with any sense would know it was all a lie or a dream. Shelby had had her fill of that. That was why she had been headed out of town tonight. Slipping away after her last shift, leaving nothing but a note to explain that it was time she started over in a place where she wasn't known as softhearted Shelby. That was the best way to make an exit from the Crosspoint Café once and for all.

Of course, now that exit would have to wait. She tucked the note into the old backpack she'd had since she was a teen, and looked for something to keep her busy. "I'll make coffee."

"You think this will take long?" Jax called out as she hurried off. "I have plans."

"I hope those plans include watching the baby for the next few minutes, while I do this." Shelby dove into the task, grabbing a bright red plastic container from a shelf above the coffeemaker.

"Trust her, man. If anyone knows how to get around the old guys in town, it's Shelby Grace." Tyler took a seat at the long service counter and began swiveling back and forth on a stool.

"That so?" Jackson Stroud studied her through those piercing, narrowed eyes once again. He might have looked menacing if not for the fact that the whole time he kept one hand protectively on the side of the basket, making sure the baby didn't wriggle it off the tabletop.

"You want to get this done quickly? Then coffee is the only way to go." Shelby pulled out the carafe and held it up like she was filming a commercial for it.

The mysterious cowboy just scoffed.

She set the carafe down hard.

He tipped his head to her, as if to say he would bow to her expertise.

That small triumph buoyed her movements as she got out the filter and opened the container. With the rich aroma of coffee filling her nose, she tipped out a spoonful of grounds and said, "Sheriff Denby is not a young man. It's late. The least we can do for him is have some coffee waiting so he can tackle this case with a clear head."

"Clear head? That may be hoping for a bit much," Tyler joked.

"I was supposed to retire over a year ago." The familiar booming voice of Sheriff Andrew Denby—Sheriff Andy to the locals—echoed in the café as he appeared in the doorway. "But they can't find a replacement willing to work my hours for the amount the county budget can afford to pay. Nights like this, I don't wonder if I'll ever retire. Who are you?"

Jax held his hand out to the man, but his expression remained reserved. "Jackson Stroud. I found the basket."

"I'm sorry, Sheriff Andy, but this couldn't be helped." Shelby poured water in the machine, flipped it on, then turned to find the older man peering down into the basket on the table.

"It's not just a do-nothing job, you know." The sheriff spoke directly to Jackson Stroud, who nodded politely. "We get our share of excitement coming in off the highway. Anyone they hire needs to be a diplomat to work with the town council, a stickler to meet state and county regs, a detective and apparently—" he reached in, lifted the baby up and gave a sniff "—a diaper changer."

"Oh, Sheriff, let me take care of that." Shelby rushed forward.

"You pour the coffee. This ol' grandpa knows which end is which." The sheriff gathered baby and clean diaper and headed for the restroom, calling over his shoulder, "So no idea who the parents are? No clues? No note?"

"Nothing." Shelby set the coffee down.

"*She* had a note." Jax eyed her. "And a backpack full of stuff on her way out the door after closing up early. If you look at her face, you'll find she's been crying."

The sheriff reentered the room. He, Tyler and Jax all locked their gazes on her at once.

Shelby felt as if she'd been slapped. "What? You can't possibly have seen all that."

Sheriff Denby slipped into the restroom without any further response.

"I don't know how you do police work around here, but some people might call that a clue." Jax raised his voice to make sure the sheriff heard.

"Yeah? Well, around here, it's what we call besmirching a good woman's reputation!" Shelby came around the counter, her pace underscoring the quick clip of her irritation at what this total stranger seemed determined to pin on her. "I may be a soft touch. I may have wasted most of my life waiting for my father's dreams of raising quarter horses to pay off so he could buy us this café like he promised. I may even have thrown away three of my twenty-eight years thinking Mitch Warner would stop running around with other girls and settle down with me, but…" Her voice broke. Her heart pounded. She had never admitted all of that out loud to anyone. Pouring it out to Jackson Stroud left her feeling vulnerable but justified when she jerked her head high and concluded, "I am not the kind of girl who would have a child without being married and if I were a mother. Let me assure you, I'd never leave him or her. I'd do anything in my power to protect my baby…"

"It's a girl." Round-faced Sheriff Denby appeared with the freshly diapered infant and handed her to Shelby.

"Surprise, surprise." Jax cocked his head and crossed his arms. "No chance you knew that already?"

Shelby sighed and shook her head at the implication in his question.

"And her name is Amanda," the sheriff went on. "At least that's what it says in fancy stitching on the corner of this blanket she was wrapped up in."

"Hand-stitched, huh?" Jax looked at the corner of the blanket, then at Shelby's decorated backpack. "Any flowers on it?"

"You have got to be kidding." Shelby couldn't help but laugh as she spoke to baby Amanda to get her point across to everyone. "This guy thinks I'm your mother, sweet pea."

"Shelby Grace? A mama?" Sheriff Denby snorted out a laugh that someone else might have taken as an insult. "No way could she have had a baby and kept it a secret around here. Maybe somebody could have, but not her. We all know her story."

"I don't," Jax said in a soft tone that bordered on dangerous—but also carried interest.

"This ain't about you." Sheriff Denby moved to the counter, picked up the coffee carafe and flipped over a cup on the counter. But he didn't pour. "This is about Shelby Grace."

"Right. We agree on that, at least." Jax adjusted his hat, and the movement came off as a kind of sly tip of congrats to the sheriff for being on his side.

"What do you mean? About me how?" Shelby cradled the baby higher in her arms, but that did nothing to temper the sinking feeling in the pit of her stomach.

"Everybody in town knows your story, Shelby Grace. We all know about your daddy, about that Mitch. Some of us even know that you broke your lease and packed up all your belongings today."

"Huh?" Tyler glanced up and blinked. "You moving, Miz Shelby?"

"I don't know your story, Miss Lockhart, but I do know that *that's* an interesting development."

People were not supposed to find out this way, not by hearing it couched in supposition and gossip, and certainly not before her father. "It doesn't matter, Tyler. None of this has anything to do with me and—"

"Hold that thought right there, young lady." Sheriff Denby flipped a waiting coffee mug over on the counter and helped himself to a steaming hot cup. "There is a more than passing fair chance that whoever left that baby on the doorstep, when you were here closing up all by your lonesome, left her here for *you* to find."

"Makes sense to me." Jax turned toward the door, then looked at Tyler. "You said someone tried to steal gas from the station tonight. Did they happen to be driving a silver SUV?"

"Uh, no. Actually, when I looked up and saw a faded red Mustang slide up to the pump, I thought it was Mitch come to see Miz Shelby. So I stopped paying attention until they took off fast. That's when I thought maybe they'd filled up and run off without paying, but turns out their credit card had been denied and they didn't get a drop."

"Mitch?" Jax leaned one elbow on the counter, gave Shelby a hard look, then glanced at the baby. "Any particular reason this Mitch might have come by tonight and not hung around to talk to you face-to-face? He a *friend* of yours?"

"An *ex...friend*," Shelby said, oddly defensive in this man's presence. Still, she searched the baby's face for any similarity to Mitch, who she had forgiven more than once for cheating on her.

The man stared her down with an expression that made her feel he knew all about Mitch and his cheating ways, though that would be impossible. Wouldn't it?

"This Mitch wouldn't be the kind of *ex-friend* who might think you'd be a good person to raise his child, would he?" Jax asked, sounding far too matter-of-fact for that kind of question.

"The last thing Mitch Warner would have wanted was to be a daddy," Sheriff Denby snorted.

Shelby tucked the baby in closer, as if that might conceal how strongly her heart was beating at the very idea that Mitch might have done something like this. "Of course, we are conveniently overlooking the possibility that the baby was left by someone who doesn't even *know* me. Someone *we* don't know, for that matter."

"Like me?" The man with the cool eyes and the quick smile cocked his head at her.

"I'm just saying that we all know one another around here. You just showed up." At the worst time. Or maybe the best, if he had no connection to tiny Amanda. "To-night, of all nights."

"You want to know who I am, Miss Shelby Grace Lockhart? I'm a man who served four years with the Greater Dallas police force." He reached into his back pocket and withdrew his wallet, glanced down at it, grimaced slightly and put it back. "At least I used to. Now I'm, for all intents and purposes, homeless and unemployed for the next couple of weeks."

He gave her a wistful smile that hinted he expected her to find that notion so preposterous, she would have to laugh. She didn't know whether to smile or shake her head at that.

He nodded at her nonresponse. "You got me. I'm pretty much the most likely suspect in your child abandonment scenario."

"Yup." Andy Denby set the coffee cup down on the counter without a drop ever going in his mouth. "Not trying to be punitive. Got to consider what's right and best for little Amanda. My wife is the town's only physician, so it makes sense we get the child to my house to be checked over."

"So that means…" Jax narrowed his eyes and held out his hands like a man waiting to carry out an order.

"That makes it official. This is a case. I'll call in what details we have tonight, see if there are missing children reports that might be connected. Whatever else needs to be done can wait till morning." The sheriff turned to grab a to-go cup and poured his untouched coffee into it as he half spoke, half yawned. "C'mon, Shelby

Grace. The old doc will be tickled pink to have you and that little one stay with us for the night."

"Stay? In Sunnyside?" Her mind raced. She had planned to be long gone by morning, to have begun a whole new life. "Can't you just take the baby and…"

"And what?" Sheriff Denby took the emptied ceramic cup around behind the counter and disappeared long enough to bend down and drop it in the dirty dishpan. He motioned to her, then to her backpack. "Allow you to leave town before we get statements and figure out what's best for little Amanda?"

Shelby held her breath. How had the sheriff known she was fleeing town tonight? Had she been that obvious? She turned to Jackson Stroud, as if she actually hoped that somehow he would spring to her rescue. That was his style, right? If he was telling the truth, that he had come over to save a basket he thought held kittens, then why wouldn't he save her?

The man in the Stetson stepped forward. "So that's it? I can get back on my way, then?"

Cowboys. Shelby let out a huff. You couldn't trust them, at least not to do anything but think of their own hides.

"Absolutely…*not.*" The sheriff put the lid on his to-go cup with a soft click. "It's late. I can't call around to find somebody to put you up, so I'm asking nice. Will you just bunk at the Truck Stop Inn for the night so we can sort this out with clear heads tomorrow morning?"

"I can let you in." Tyler started toward the back of the building, motioning. "It ain't fancy, but there's a couple rooms with cots and a shower that we rent out to truckers by the night."

"Tell Miss Delta to bill the department for it." Sheriff Denby clapped his hands together, then motioned for Shelby to hurry up and get her things together. "As of now, this is an official investigation. I'll thank you not to leave town, Stroud, until after we speak again."

"I was only joking about being homeless and unemployed. I have a job waiting for me in Miami. I was on my way there tonight to find a place to live and get the lay of the land before I start work." Jax followed behind Tyler. "I can't stay here indefinitely. I have—"

Denby gave the stranger a hard look that cut him right off. But when the man got even with the sheriff, it did not escape Shelby's keen eye that the older man added something to the conversation that made the wandering cowboy's wide shoulders stiffen. He glanced back at Shelby and the baby.

The world seemed to stand still for a moment.

Then Jax nodded to no one in particular and said, "I guess I can spare some time. But as soon as I have nothing more to offer this case, I need to get on my way."

Chapter Three

Jax rolled onto his side. The whole framework of the old cot creaked. When he'd climbed between the scratchy, bleached brilliant white sheets last night, he hadn't expected to get much sleep. He thought he would never get comfortable or be able to quiet his mind after the day's events. But the minute his head had hit the pillow, the prayer he had shared with Shelby had come echoing back to him, and a sweet peace had washed over him. The next thing he knew, the dim light of the new day was creeping through the crack where the shade did not quite meet the windowsill.

He checked his cell phone for the time and swung his legs over the side of the bed. Head bowed, he rubbed his fists into his eyes. Tyler had said that both the café and the convenience mart opened at six in the morning. That meant, he calculated, he had twenty-five minutes to get ready for…

For what? A few hours ago, his course had been set. If you'd asked him then, he'd have told you without hesitation that he'd be in Miami this morning. He'd be scouting out apartments, looking over the exclusive gated community where, on the first of next month, he'd start his job as head of security. Now he didn't even know what to expect beyond getting up and getting dressed.

That his lack of control in this new situation didn't have him on edge was not like him at all. Jax was a man always one step ahead of everyone else. He pressed his eyes shut tightly. For a moment he considered praying for guidance, but in the end he decided what he really needed was determination. He set his own way, and his way was toward Miami before the end of the day.

He sighed as the peace of last night turned into a weight pressing down on his shoulders. That weight did not lift as he cleaned up with the toiletries Tyler had gathered for him last night. He'd feel better if he could put on clean clothes, but that would have to wait until he reached Florida tonight.

He walked into the Shoppers' Emporium part of the building in time to see the spectacular sunrise over the wide-open Texas landscape, framed by a large plate-glass window. It was the loveliest thing he'd seen in a long time.

"Make that the second-loveliest thing," he murmured to himself as Shelby Grace Lockhart suddenly stepped into view from around the corner in the parking lot. Her hair was windswept, her expression determined, and both her hands gripped the handle of a baby carrier.

"Miss Delta?" Shelby peered in with her cute little nose all but smashed against the glass. "You in there yet?"

"I'm coming. Just hold on to your—" A woman who looked to be a few years shy of sixty, with hair the color and consistency of sunburnt hay, bustled past him, then slowed. She gave him a quick once-over and cocked one penciled eyebrow. She paused long enough to plunk her fist on her bony hip and ask him, "Cowboy or trucker?"

"Cop," he said, then corrected himself. "*Ex*-cop, that is."

Shelby knocked on the door. "Miss Delta? I'm kind of in a hurry. You'll never believe what happened last night."

"And I can't wait to hear all about it," Delta murmured in Jax's direction even as she pivoted and went to unlock the front door. "Shelby Grace, where did you get that sweet little fellow?"

"It's a girl," Shelby corrected at the exact same time the words left Jax's lips. Their perfect timing didn't take the edge off her pointed tone as she added, "*Someone* left her outside the café last night."

Shelby gave Jax an unyielding stare. In return, Jax gave Shelby…the biggest grin he'd ever grinned. Which wasn't saying much, since he never grinned. Or he never used to. But there he was, unable to stop himself.

"How is she doing?" he asked, his eyes on Shelby's face.

"Doc Lovey checked her out. She's in good shape, but a little underweight for what Doc thinks is a four-month-old." Shelby shifted the weight of the carrier and, in doing so, got a bit off balance.

"Doc Lovey?" Jax asked as he rushed forward and scooped the carrier up out of her hands. It felt light to him. No, it wasn't the carrier that felt light. It was him. Like that weight he had felt since plotting his getaway from here had lifted.

"Lovey. Sheriff Denby's wife. It's a nickname, but everyone around here calls her that." Miss Delta tipped her head back a bit so she could give Jax another once-over, then fixed her attention on the baby in the carrier. "Lovely is what *this* sweet thing is. What a cutie. Who could have ever left something this precious?"

"Someone who knew they were placing their baby in good hands," Jax said, almost under his breath. He met Shelby's hesitant gaze and held it until she took a deep breath and smiled.

"That's a sweet idea, I guess," Shelby whispered.

But? She did not say it, or even hint that there was more to say, but Jax felt it. Something else was going on with Shelby Grace Lockhart. Anyone else might have prodded, peppering her with questions to find out more, but Jax knew that people's true motivations showed in their actions, not their words. So he held his tongue and waited.

Shelby glanced over her shoulder toward the café, then down at baby Amanda in the carrier, which Jax held easily by the handle. "But I can't…I don't have it in me anymore to take on one more person's broken promises."

"Promises?" he asked softly.

"A baby left on her own in the dark of night?" Her eyes met his. Her hair swept over her shoulder as she shook her head. "If that doesn't say someone some-where broke a promise and now wants someone else—"

"You," he interrupted.

"Me." She nodded in agreement. "Now someone wants me to do what everyone knows Shelby Grace does so well. Pick up the slack. Put the pieces back together. Always be there. I just don't think I can do it anymore."

He wanted to speak to her of faith. Of knowing where to find strength. Of what it felt like to be a child caught in the middle of a world with no Shelby Graces in it. Instead, he swallowed his opinion and supported her with a quiet "yeah" and a nod of his head.

She shuffled her feet, then squinted toward the large window, where the sun had begun to shine in and create shadows around them.

Clearly she wanted to get moving. But where? And why? None of his business, of course. Under other circumstances, he would have let it go. He studied her profile, the curve of her cheek. The shadows under her eyes told of a sleepless night. He couldn't let it go—not with the simple question Sheriff Denby had asked him echoing in his mind. *Why Shelby Grace Lockhart?*

"I can't believe there's nothing this little sweetheart needs," Delta cooed as she gave the baby's head a pat. "I'm going to go see what I can find."

"Don't trouble yourself, Miss Delta." Shelby raised her hand in a halfhearted attempt to slow the juggernaut that was Miss Delta of Delta's Truck Stop Inn. "Doc Lovey got us diapers and formula from the county health department. After I help the sheriff look for any signs of who might have left the baby, I volunteered to take her to social services over in West…more…land."

Shelby's shoulders sagged as the older woman hurried away, rattling off a list of things she wanted to gather for the baby.

"Here kind of early, aren't you?" he finally asked. "I don't see the sheriff anywhere around."

"There's something I have to do at the café before then."

"Oh?" He narrowed his eyes. It was a simple technique to speak little and act like you expected an answer. Oftentimes people complied without even knowing why. Other times they hesitated, then felt compelled to fill the silence, usually with the very information Jax needed.

Shelby did neither. She took the carrier and settled it on the counter. In doing so, she put her back to Jax. "Delta, will you watch the baby for a few minutes? I'll come back for her just as soon as I—"

Jax clamped his hand down on the woman's shoulder, partly in reassurance, partly to tell her he would not be so easily dismissed. "Don't bother. I'll bring her over."

Shelby whipped her head around. Her shoulder went from strained and tense under his touch to stiff but confident. It was a small shift, but one that let him know she would not be intimidated by him, that she had the grit to hold her own ground.

"You?" Miss Delta poked her head out from behind a round display of candy a few feet away. She gave Jax a once-over, then a twice-over. "Pardon my saying so, but you hardly look like the babysitting type."

"Foster care," Shelby said before Jax could come to his own defense. She pressed the handle of a baby carrier, labeled Property of the Sunnyside, Texas, Police Dept., into his hand. "Meet me in the café in a few minutes."

Somewhere in the shop, something fell off the shelf. As soon as Shelby left, Miss Delta tiptoed from behind that shelf and whispered, "You gonna let her do that? Take that baby to Westmoreland?"

The question, and the implication that Jax had any say over what Shelby did with the child, caught him off guard. "Is Westmoreland really that bad?"

"You know what I mean. Take her to…" Delta hurried over to cover the baby's ears, and even then she spoke in a whisper. "Social services."

Baby Amanda gurgled.

Jax's heart clenched. He had been eight when his mom died and he'd been taken to social services. It was a moment he hadn't thought of in years, and yet he was not foolish enough to think it hadn't affected him every day of his life.

"What choice do I have?" He wasn't asking rhetorically. He really hoped she had another suggestion.

"I asked you first," she said, in a way that left the impression that if she did have some ideas, she wasn't going to just blurt them out to him. He got that. He was not only an outsider, but he was a total stranger, too. Yet her choice to keep her thoughts to herself actually made his opinion of her go up a couple more notches.

Jax didn't say a word to that effect. But he did turn to stand next to Miss Delta, looking down at the innocent in the carrier. After a moment, he looked the older woman in the eyes and said softly, "I know I'm a stranger here, but I don't think for one moment that Shelby Grace or Sheriff Denby would let this child go anywhere that wasn't the right place for her to be."

"I know that, young man. I just hope you do, as well." Miss Delta nodded, then looked down at the baby. She touched the child's head and bent to give her a kiss on the forehead, which left a bright pink smudge. "You said you were an *ex*-cop?"

"Yes, ma'am. On my way from four years of service in the Dallas area to a dream job doing private security for the ultrarich in Florida."

"Dream job?" She stood back, squinted one eye shut and pressed her lips together to make sure he knew she had sized him up good. "For a man like you? Doing the bidding of the 'ultrarich' sounds more like a nightmare."

"It's helping people without the complications of… the people." That was as best as he could describe it on the spot. He had to admit, the overly simplified explanation didn't make him proud of his choice.

Miss Delta homed in on that right away. She shook her head, causing the necklaces she wore to jangle softly. "*That's* what you have your heart set on? Spending your days as a hired *helper*?"

He repositioned his grip on the baby carrier and his boots on the concrete floor and assured her, "It is."

"In Miami, Florida?"

"Got a contract that says that's where I'm supposed to be."

"Yet here you stand, at the door of the Shoppers' Emporium in Sunnyside, Texas." She narrowed her eyes and tapped the toe of her shoe, which was much too fancy for standing on your feet all day.

"What?" Jax demanded, knowing the woman wanted to say more.

"Nothing." She gave an exaggerated sigh and shook her head. "Only, I wonder if you ever considered that you might just be where you are supposed to be already."

Jax froze for a moment to try to piece together what she meant by that. He was just a guy who had happened by, right? He didn't have any reason to get involved. And yet…

He leaned down to wipe the lipstick off Amanda's head. "I'll take that under consideration, ma'am."

"I believe you will." Miss Delta reached out, grabbed his chin and drew his face close enough to plant a big ol' kiss on his whiskered cheek. "I really do believe you will."

That was how he came to walk through the door of the café, swiping at his cheek with the sleeve of his jacket, carrying a foundling baby, grinning and looking for Shelby. Questions about and reactions to the little one in the carrier began flying at him the second he walked into the café from the few patrons who had begun to shuffle in and settle down for their morning meal.

"What a sweetie."

"How old…?"

"Just precious!"

Questions and reactions to the little one in the carrier began flying at him the second he walked into the café from the few patrons who had begun to shuffle in and settle down for their morning meal. Jax knew they all meant well, but being the center of all this attention was not his style. He was more a stand back and observe kind of guy. Yet with each new set of eyes trained on him, he wanted more and more to retreat.

Retreat? When had that *ever* been his reaction to anything?

Since he had someone to protect, was his instinctive response.

Jax raised the baby up, forced a wincing smile as he moved away from the prying gazes and began looking around for Shelby to help him out. She wasn't at a table. Or behind the counter.

"You cannot do this, Shelby Grace. Not now!" The tense, stressed twang of a man's voice made Jax turn. He spotted Shelby through the opening to the kitchen, arguing with a man with faded blond hair pulled back in a ponytail.

He couldn't help thinking of Denby's concern that whoever had left the baby had basically targeted Shelby Grace Lockhart for a reason. Old beliefs twisted in Jax's gut. Emotion and agendas based on selfishness sometimes made people do desperate things.

He thought of Delta's cryptic advice that he was where he needed to be. Suddenly being here, with this baby and Shelby, felt all wrong.

Without hesitation, Jax headed for the swinging kitchen door.

"I can't do it anymore," Shelby argued, her own

voice pitched high with a mix of pleading and anxiety. "You're going to have to find a way to make the payment or start riding a horse to work."

"Shelby, hon, talk sense." The man reached out for her.

Jax found his hand, the one not holding the handle of the baby carrier, doing the same.

Shelby evaded the man's grasp with a quick duck of her shoulder, and in doing so, she also put herself out of Jax's reach.

"I am talking sense. For the first time since I realized, deep down, that you were never going to make a go of the ranch, and I was never going to own this café." Shelby turned to look back, raised her hand, then brushed away a stray curl that had caught on her eyelashes. "I can't tell you how much I wanted to believe, to go on dreaming that some day…but last night I looked around and realized that someday isn't coming. We've given it all we've got, and we have to face the fact that we can't do it, Dad."

"Dad?"

Shelby turned to look at Jax.

Before she could tear into him for listening in on a private—if intriguing—conversation, Jax said, "I was actually thinking it might be smart to start looking around for any clues now, before too many people disturb things."

She sighed, then gave him a single nod. For just a moment, he thought she might cave in to her father's wishes and stay. She certainly wasn't quick to rush off, and her tone carried the heaviness of resignation as she finally agreed, "You're right. Let's go out the back way and walk around to the front. The sooner we get this behind us, the sooner I can get on with what's ahead of me."

Chapter Four

With one hand firmly wrapped around Amanda's carrier handle, Jax hustled them outside, where the aroma of pancakes and bacon followed them. The damp warmth of the café kitchen met the fresh morning air, and Shelby took a deep breath.

"Guess that old saying is true," he said with a quiet intensity. "Everything looks different in the light of day."

Shelby scanned the view behind the café. It all looked familiar to her. Too familiar. Sunnyside, Texas, from any vantage point, was not the view she'd expected to greet her this morning. She turned to fix her gaze on the tall figure at her side, now holding the baby easily against his chest. That sight *was* different.

He glanced her way and shook his head, a smile playing over his lips.

Her heart fluttered. "I…I don't know…what you mean."

"This changes everything." He motioned toward the back parking lot.

Shelby frowned. "It does?"

"It was so late when I got here last night that most of these houses already had their lights out." He narrowed his eyes, his gaze fixed on the row of neat little homes across the small lot and a strip of grassy ground beyond it. "I didn't realize all these houses were so close back here."

"Oh. Well, it's a small town. Everyone practically lives on top of everyone else. At least it feels like that some days." Shelby's shoulders ached, and her head began to throb. "You said it changes everything?"

"Sure. Last night I was thinking that whoever left the baby came by car, so they made quite a trip in order to reach you. But with people living this close? Maybe it wasn't you but the café that was the draw for the baby. They left her someplace they could watch to make sure she was okay."

A cloud passed over the rising sun. Shelby shivered.

"I'm going to look around and see what I can find." He settled the baby carrier down on the wooden slats at her feet and gave her a nod before heading out.

He expected her to stay put and watch over the foundling. Clearly the man did not understand that Shelby was done doing what other people expected. It took her only a moment to bend down and unsnap the safety latches holding Amanda in place. She lifted the baby up and cuddled her close, even as she headed to the steps to follow Jax onto the gravel that served as an employee parking lot.

"No one in Sunnyside would have been able to hide

a pregnancy, much less a baby, for three months, let me assure you."

"You honestly think there are no secrets in this town?" He looked back over his shoulder at her. "Would you say everybody here knows all there is to know about you, Shelby Grace?"

She pulled up short. Her stomach clenched. It was like he was looking right through her. She thought of the note she had written last night, of her deepest fear, which she was sure no other living soul knew or would understand.

"You know who owns all three of these vehicles?" Jax motioned toward the dust-covered blue pickup truck, the ten-year-old minivan and the lime-green convertible parked side by side in the lot.

Shelby forced her mind back to the task at hand—gathering information to find whoever had left Amanda. "Um, the convertible is Miss Delta's, the minivan is mine and the truck—"

"Is also yours," he said, finishing for her, sounding somewhere between speculative and show-offy at having come to that conclusion. "That's the payment you need your dad to take on, I'm guessing."

"I bought the van so I could cater some local events once I saved up enough to… Well, it doesn't matter now. My dad's truck bit the dust, and he couldn't get a loan for a new one. So good ol' Shelby got one for him."

"Good ol' Shelby," he muttered as he strode on from the back parking lot to the side of the building. He kicked the toe of his boot at a clump of grass, then lifted his head and studied where the paved customer lot ended just by the edge of the deck.

The baby squirmed in her arms and made a soft, fussy sound, pushing at the blanket flap swept over her head and wadded against her now-warm pink cheek.

"Do you really think we might find something helpful out here?" Shelby rearranged the blanket and baby so that Amanda could wave her arms freely. That allowed the sun to shine on her sweet, round face.

"It's not so much about thinking at this point." He raised his hand to his temple, his expression a mask of concentration. He was completely immersed in the moment. Cool. Focused. Intense. "Trying to outthink the situation is how people jump to conclusions. That can tempt them to try to prove themselves right instead of trying to find the truth."

Shelby glanced over her shoulder, back at the café, where she had thought through her own situation hour after hour. She had felt trapped in a role not of her own making, unable to spread her wings. She had obsessed over the fear that she would never own her own business. That no man would ever love her enough to be faithful to her. That Mitch Warner was the best she would ever do and that she would end up like her father, always chasing a dream forever out of her reach. As she stood here now in the daylight, Jax's words went straight to her heart. Had she been trying to prove her conclusions about life in Sunnyside, or had she been seeking the truth? "Man, you're good at this. Anyone ever tell you that?"

He glanced up and met her eyes. A smile tugged

at one corner of his mouth. "I haven't even done anything yet."

"But you're going to." Shelby had no idea how she knew that, but she knew it beyond the shadow of a doubt. After a lifetime spent around men who didn't seem able to do anything, she *knew*. "So just what is it that you're going to do?"

"Right now?" He lifted one shoulder, then let it down. "I'm gonna look around."

"Oh." That should not have disappointed her as much as it did. "So you don't have any hunches?"

Before he could answer, Amanda sneezed.

"Oh! God bless you, sweetheart," Shelby whispered.

Jax turned, and his expression warmed as he, too, mouthed "God bless you" to their tiny charge. No sooner had the words left his lips than his shoulders stiffened and his voice went hard. "No. No hunches. Other than that whoever left that little cutie did it in a hurry."

"In a hurry like someone committing a crime?" She settled the baby on her hip and made a quick swipe to wipe the tiny pink-tipped nose. Once she had thought of it, the theory came quickly to her lips. "Like somebody kidnapping a baby and then panicking and deciding to ditch it somewhere?"

He frowned.

"Or in a hurry like someone ripping off a Band-Aid?" she asked, feeling a bit like she should have led with that. "You know it's going to hurt, so you do it as quickly as possible. Get it over with."

"Yeah. Yeah, like that Band-Aid thing," he muttered as he scanned the tall grass, his eyes narrowed to slits.

"I don't think it's a kidnapping case. I'm sure Denby checked to see if there are any alerts for a missing infant and acted on that right away."

"Sheriff Andy did go back to the office last night." She watched Jax a moment, not sure what to do. Just twenty-four hours ago, she had resolved to take charge of her life and had thought she might actually pull it off. She might really leave Sunnyside. Now? Now she needed to ask Jax a question she realized she probably should have asked herself yesterday, when she had packed up her few personal belongings and had told her landlord to keep the cleaning deposit. "What are you looking for, exactly?"

"I don't know, *exactly.*" He reached up in a gesture Shelby recognized as a man adjusting his cowboy hat to shade his eyes. But there was no hat, so at the last second the man rubbed his palm lightly through his dark hair. "When people get in a big hurry, they don't think straight. They come up with a half-baked plan and carry it through before they get cold feet."

Shelby shifted her feet nervously back and forth.

"That's when they make mistakes."

"Then again, something this monumental surely had a lot of thought behind it." Shelby pulled her shoulders up. His comment was not aimed at her or her emotionally charged decision to turn her back on everything she knew. Still, it put her on the defensive. "It wasn't necessarily an impulse."

"No." He shook his head. "A woman abandoning a baby in the night, even with the most trustworthy person in the whole town, isn't something she's going to plot out."

The most trustworthy person in the whole town. On one hand, hearing him describe her that way sent a shimmer of pride and happiness through her. On the other hand, it seemed a pretty improbable expectation to live up to. Shelby looked at baby Amanda, then at Jax, and in doing so, she knew. She *wanted* to live up to it. She wanted to be worthy of the trust placed in her. "You're so sure it was a woman? Her mother?"

"Maybe someone else was with her, but there is the footprint of a woman's shoe in the mud." He knelt down and touched the ground, then stood again with something small and pink in his hand. "And I believe with all my being she was the mom. A kidnapper wouldn't have brought this."

"She had to be so desperate," Shelby whispered, her heart aching at the sight of the floppy home-sewn bunny in his hand.

"Had to be," he said in a way that sounded like he had some kind of personal stake in that conclusion. He stood and walked over to where Shelby stood holding Amanda. "To do this, she clearly didn't think she had anyone in her life she could turn to…except you."

He held out his hand with the humble handmade toy in it for Shelby to take.

Shelby hesitated, then reached out, her hand almost trembling.

Her fingers brushed his.

For less than a second, he held on to the toy. Shelby couldn't explain how, but much like when they had prayed together over Amanda last night, she felt a connection to this cowboy who had walked into her life when she had needed it the least—and Amanda had needed it most.

Without warning, Jax loosened his grip. The rabbit slid through his large, rough hands, the long ears dragging through his blunt, calloused fingers.

It felt like a passing of the responsibility to Shelby. Jax had found the baby. He had stayed long enough to help Sheriff Denby. He had found what clues he could. The rest was up to her.

Shelby turned the crudely sewn animal over in her hand and shook her head. "You're right. There's no one else to take this on here. No one except good ol' softhearted Shelby Grace Lockhart."

They had waited another twenty minutes for Denby to show up at the café before Shelby's father remembered to tell them the sheriff had called right after the pair had gone out to the back parking lot. The town's deputy on duty had had to go out to oversee a dispute between two neighbors, and Denby needed to stay close to the office. He wanted them to bring Amanda there to give their statements.

"A desperate mother who thought of Shelby as her only resource?" Sheriff Denby came around to the front of the large wooden desk in his cluttered office to peer into the face of the baby in Shelby's arms before he leaned back to make a seat of the edge of the desk. "I pretty much came to that conclusion last night."

With Shelby settled into the only chair in the room,

aside from the one behind the desk, Jax leaned one shoulder against the wall. He crossed his arms. "Then why didn't you share your theory last night, instead of asking me—"

"Because I was hoping you'd come at this with a fresh set of eyes, Mr. Stroud. Or should I call you Officer?"

"Just Jax is enough." Jax held up his hand. "I'm a civilian now."

"No such thing. Once a lawman, always a lawman." The older man groaned a bit as he rose from his perch on the corner of the desk. He winced and straightened slowly. "Of all people, I know how hard it is to walk away from the calling."

"The *calling?*" Jax swept his gaze over the walls of the office, which were covered with plaques, framed photos and citations that recounted a history of service. Just standing here humbled and touched him. His few short years on the force paled in comparison to this kind of work, and his new job? Well, it didn't compare at all.

He tried to tell himself he'd still be helping others in Miami. But he couldn't stay convinced of that when he turned his head and found himself looking at Shelby cradling Amanda. How could patrolling the playground of those who could afford anything in the world compare to standing up for and protecting those who had nowhere else to turn?

"I don't know." Jax shook his head. "Maybe you're right. Maybe it's hard for some people to leave the life of a lawman behind. A calling, like you say. But me?"

"You?" Shelby made a big show of rolling her eyes and laughing at Jax's weak protest.

Amanda fussed at the sudden, albeit soft, outburst.

Shelby didn't miss a beat. She curled the baby close and rose deftly from her chair. Her feet did a *scuff, scuff, shuffle* over the old floor, lulling the baby into woozy contentment, and with hushed words she still managed to knock Jax off his guard and send him reeling with her insight. "You mean the would-be kitten rescuer just rolling through town who let himself get waylaid into a situation with a lost baby? Or the guy who got up at dawn to help with an investigation and make sure everything was okay?"

"Okay, okay. You got me pegged, Shelby Grace." Jax held both hands up and laughed. He turned around to face her.

She pulled up short in her pacing, stopping just inches away from him, with baby Amanda in between them.

"You got me," Jax repeated barely above a whisper.

She blinked her clear blue eyes in an expression that seemed half startled, half flustered. She started to step to the side.

Jax did the same. "I…here…let me…"

Neither seemed able to complete a thought, much less an action or a sentence.

Sheriff Denby did not have that problem. "Good. We're all clear on that. Then everything's settled, right?"

"Settled?" Jax repeated the word hardly above a murmur. Never in his whole life had he felt settled—nor did he want to feel that way. But standing here, looking at Shelby holding Amanda…

Denby clapped his hands. "Let's make it official."

"Official?" Jax said.

"Yes, sir." Denby went around the desk and whipped open one of the drawers. As he fished around inside it, he said, "I'm going to deputize you, son. So you can escort Shelby and this baby over to Westmoreland."

"You're going to what?" Jax stepped back without thinking. He smashed into a row of awards, which slid sideways and fell forward. He had to act fast to save them from crashing to the floor. "Why?"

"Why?" Sheriff Denby chuckled as he pulled out a badge. "Think a hotshot lawman from… Where did you say you were from, son?"

"I'm not from anywhere. Until yesterday, I lived in Dallas. As soon as I leave Sunnyside, I'm going to live in Miami for a while."

"Dallas," Denby said as he pulled out a file and slapped it on the desk. "That's the one I called to check you out."

"You what?"

"Ran your license plate last night, after I left here. Made some calls." The white-haired sheriff met Jax's eyes, almost in a challenge at first. A pause, then a slow, kindly smile followed. "Didn't think I'd trust you with our Shelby without checking you out first, did you?"

Jax looked at the woman standing at his side with her mouth hanging open, those fire-spitting eyes fixed on the man behind the desk. He laughed. "Blame you? I'd have done the same things myself."

"I know you would have, son. That's why I'm asking you to step up now and help us all out." Denby opened the file and pointed at the paper. "Sign here, and I'll swear you in."

"What do you mean, trust him with me?" Shelby came forward. If she hadn't been holding Amanda, Jax got the sense she would have pushed her way around the desk and met Denby nose to nose, or as close to his nose as she could get beyond his rounded stomach. "I can take care of myself, Sheriff Andy."

"I'm sure you can, but for now your job is to take care of Amanda, so just for today I think you need someone else to look after you. I can't leave the office, so…" Denby snatched up a pen and offered it to Jax. "Just for one day. For Shelby."

She shook her head. "I don't need—"

For Shelby.

Jax took the pen and signed his name, even knowing that somewhere along the line he was going to pay for letting himself get involved like this.

Chapter Five

Shelby fidgeted with the seat belt, when she really wanted to stretch back and check the straps holding Amanda's car seat in place. Why she thought she would know how to buckle in the carrier better than Jax, she didn't know. In fact, as far as babies went, the man seemed to have a lot more experience than she did. Slyly, she glanced over at him from under a spiral of hair that had fallen over her forehead and cheek.

"Ready?" he asked in that deep, resonant Texas drawl of his.

"For what?" she almost whispered. She would have *had* to have whispered it, because meeting his gaze in these close quarters had all but taken her breath away.

The minivan lurched forward. "Let's do this."

He had not made up some reason to make her drive, as her dad would have. He did not whine about the one-hundred-twenty-mile round trip or mutter about how long it might take with the social services department. Her ex, Mitch, would do that every time they spent more than a few minutes doing something that didn't interest him. No, Jackson Stroud just did what needed to be done.

Shelby marveled not just at that, but also at how impressed she was. She wanted to tell him so but couldn't help thinking that "Thanks for doing what you do" was an odd compliment. So as they passed the sign reading Buffalo Betty's Chuck Wagon Ranch House, 19 Miles, she blurted out the first thing that came to her lips. "You look good behind the wheel of a minivan."

"I what?" He gave her a sideways glance, then fixed his cool dark eyes on the road ahead and gave a deep-throated chuckle. "Shelby Grace, are you… Was that your way of flirting with me? Because if it was, I've heard better."

"I wasn't…that is… I didn't…" Shelby gulped in the big breath she had been about to take.

His chuckle opened into a warm, soft laugh. "Relax. No man wants to hear he looks good driving a minivan. I'm just having some fun with you for saying it."

"Fun. That must be why I misunderstood." She took a deep breath and slouched back against the gray upholstered seat. "It's been so long since I've done anything truly fun, I'm afraid I don't even recognize it when I see it anymore."

"Maybe that explains it."

"Explains what?"

"The sadness on your face last night, when I first looked into your eyes."

"Oh, that. Actually, I…" She didn't owe him an explanation. Her whole life had built up to that moment when she had finally decided she needed to get out of Sunnyside, to start fresh somewhere else. Somewhere where nobody thought of her as softhearted Shelby and did things like leave their infants in her care. She thought of the note she had written detailing her feelings. A swirl of emotions followed and carried with it the memory of that first instant that she'd laid eyes on Jax. Then of praying over Amanda with him. How had all of that led to this?

She turned her head to watch the familiar landscape slide by for a moment before she decided the best course was to change the subject. "What happened to your cowboy hat?"

"Left it back at the Truck Stop Inn. Won't be wearing it where I'm going, so I thought…" He left that thought unfinished. "What happened to you last night that had you crying?"

Shelby looked out the passenger-door window, not wanting him to see how much the directness of the question had thrown her. "I thought cowboys never went anywhere without their hats. Where would you be going that you wouldn't need it?"

"I don't wear my hat all the time, because I'm not that kind of cowboy. Like Sheriff Denby rightly observed, I'm the Dallas lawman type of cowboy. Or I was. I've got a job waiting for me in Miami. Head of security for a community of elite homes." He rattled the answers off in an emotionless drone. But his tone did lighten as he added, "There. Does that answer all your questions?"

Not by a long shot. Where this man was concerned, it seemed like each new thing she learned only raised *more* questions. She got the feeling that pushing for more answers would only irritate him. Shelby resigned herself to the idea that she would probably never know much about the man beside her. She nodded. "Yes. Thanks for humoring me."

A second sign, this one much bigger and painted in garish hues, loomed ahead on the side of the road. *Breakfast All Day Long at Buffalo Betty's Chuck Wagon Ranch House! 5 Miles, Endless Smiles Ahead.*

"You're welcome," Jax said. "Now maybe you can return the favor and humor me. Because I've got a burning question I've got to ask."

Shelby tensed. She didn't think she could take another question about what had led her to that point in the café last night. One more, and she might just spill her guts and start sobbing over the things she felt she'd never have: love, a home, a family of her own and control over her future. Just thinking about it all made her eyes moist with unshed tears. "Oh, Jax, I don't know—"

"What in the world is a Buffalo Betty, and what about her chuck wagon and ranch house is going to make me smile?" He jerked his thumb over his shoulder in the direction of the sign they had just passed. "Endlessly, no less!"

That was not the question he had intended to ask her, and she knew it. A wave of relief washed over Shelby at his willingness to let her off the hook. How many times had other people used her vulnerability to press their advantage, to get her to go along with their wishes? The fact that Jax saw her turmoil and gave her a way out made her words practically tumble out over each other as she explained, "It's a local attraction. No, I take that back. It's *the* local attraction. A theme restaurant that serves bison, among other things, with a general store, play park and a handful of friendlyish buffalo on the grounds—fenced off away from the visitors, of course. But there is one big moth-eaten old thing that you can pet and feed."

"I don't know whether to ask you just how many buffalo you think you can scoop into a handful, or to make sure I heard right. You can both eat and feed buffalo there?"

"I guess I never thought of it that way." Shelby laughed. "I haven't been there since I was a kid."

"Then we should go now." He had already veered off into the lane to exit as he said it.

They pulled into the parking lot, found a spot and shut the engine off.

"Now? Shouldn't we be getting Amanda to the authorities?" Shelby's protest might have seemed more urgent if she hadn't said it while gathering the baby's things so they could hop out of the minivan the second the engine stopped.

"Technically, since Sheriff Denby deputized me, Amanda *is* with the authorities. And I have it on good authority that it will be in everyone's best interest to stop." He slammed the door shut firmly, as if emphasizing that no further discussion was needed.

Shelby smiled.

That's what he'd done it for, Jax thought as they took the more scenic of the walkways leading from the parking lot to the restaurant proper. He'd disrupted the whole trip just in the hopes that he could make Shelby smile.

"Oh, look, there's the old buffalo. I'm going to get something to feed it. Can you hold Amanda a sec?" She handed the child off to him like they had done the exchange a thousand times.

She trusted him. So much so that she didn't even hesitate. This, in turn, made Jax smile.

Shelby rushed off toward a huge woolly beast standing stock-still behind a wooden fence.

Amanda kicked and wriggled in his arms, and Jax looked down at her. "What?"

Another kick.

"I saw tears in her eyes. My brain said 'Fix it.' That's all. And by the way, I do not have to justify myself to someone whose side of the conversation consists of cooing and milk bubbles." He reached into his pocket to pull out a tissue from the wad he'd tucked away for just this situation, and cleaned off a fresh glob of spit from Amanda's chin.

"Here, let me have that." Shelby was at his side in a heartbeat.

"I am perfectly capable of cleaning up a baby's—"

"For the buffalo." Shelby whisked the tissue paper from his fingers and motioned for him to follow.

"It's a mechanical buffalo." Jax laughed when he got close enough to see it. "I had thought it was a bad idea to let people hand-feed a real one."

"Watch! It vacuums the trash right out of your hand." Shelby placed the tissue in her flattened palm, and with a whoosh, it disappeared.

Shelby laughed.

Which made Jax laugh.

Which made Amanda gurgle.

"She laughed!" Shelby pointed at the baby. "It was an itty-bitty baby laugh, but she did it."

"She's too young."

"She's advanced for her age."

"Everybody thinks their baby is a genius, don't they?" A kindly older woman leaned in to peer at Amanda, then raised her wrinkle-framed eyes to Jax and said, "Of course, in your case, I am absolutely certain it's true. Such a bright baby."

"She looks like you," the woman's slightly younger companion said to Jax as she peered at Amanda.

"Do you think?" The first woman leaned back and shifted her scrutiny from Jax to Amanda, then to Shelby. "I'd say she looks more like her mother."

"She has his dark hair," her companion countered, then, as a seeming afterthought, smiled kindly at Shelby and added, "But she does have your beautiful blue eyes."

Shelby shook her head and held up one hand. "She's not—"

"She's not wearing a hat." Jax shaded the baby's eyes with his hand. "We really should get her out of the sun."

"What a blessed baby to have such a loving daddy," the younger woman said with a sigh.

"And mommy, of course," the older of the two hurried to add. Then she reached toward Amanda, paused to get a nod of approval from Jax, stroked the child's tiny hand and said with genuine warmth, "Life is short. It goes so fast. Trust me on this." She put her hand on the younger woman's shoulder. "You think I'm just looking at your baby, but I know that you're looking at *my* baby here, too. It seems no time at all since she was a baby. Enjoy every minute while you can."

Jax called out a thank-you. Why go into the whole story here and now? It would all be over and behind him soon. "Maybe we should get one of those old-timey photos taken before we hit the road."

"We? The three of us?"

"Or the two of you, if you'd rather."

"Jax, we don't know this baby…or each other, for that matter. Why would we—"

"Because life *is* short, Shelby. Amanda is blessed with us now, but that's going to be over and done with when we get to Westmoreland. It's just my way of…I don't know…"

She cocked her head. "Buying a little time?"

"If you're accusing me of something, Shelby Grace, you need to make it clear."

She didn't push it. But then, he could tell by the look on her face that she wanted to; she just wasn't sure how he'd take it. Or maybe she wasn't sure how she'd deal with it if he didn't take it well.

So they went on into the restaurant in silence only broken up by small talk with the hostess who seated them promptly.

"I am starving." Jax settled the baby carrier, which he'd retrieved from the minivan, into the special chair the hostess had brought for them. "Hadn't even realized how hungry I was until I saw what I was missing."

"Missing?" Shelby fussed over Amanda before situating herself at the table.

"Dinner. Midnight snack. Breakfast." He counted off on his fingers. But when he finished that list, his heart kept ticking things off—a family, a life. "I think I'll order everything on the menu."

"I believe you." She pulled her chair out, then leaned in over the table to address him in a rushed whisper. "Not because you're that hungry, but because I think you're stalling."

He waited until Shelby had taken her seat before he asked, "Stalling?"

He wasn't denying it. He just wanted to hear why she thought he'd do it.

She paused a moment, then folded her hands on top of the table. "You don't really want to give Amanda over to the authorities, do you, Jax?"

He sank into his seat, unfurling the cloth napkin to place it in his lap. "I told you, for now I am the—"

"I know. You're 'the authority.'" Shelby spanned her hands in the air, as if reading a banner stretched across the wall. She grinned and shook her hair back from her sun-blushed cheeks. "But an authority who is reluctant to give this baby over to the non-temporary, Denby-appointed, deputy-type authorities."

He dropped the napkin into his lap, leaning forward over the table to challenge her. "I bet you couldn't say that again in a hundred tries."

She leaned in to meet that challenge. "See? More stalling. I'm right, aren't I?"

She was, and he liked it. He usually didn't like it

gh him this easily, but with
d. That was one of the rea-
through this one day they'd

the other reason. "Even an-
come back and keep this kid
it."

e tipped her head to one side.
come back?"

ess child in the seat beside
ike to get lost in the system,
t for you. "That's what I'm

s hand back through his hair.
at much thought. His whole
he'd dreamt of a day when
nd give him a family. "Then
ce for a real family. We help
pport. We help her choose a
ot leaving the baby hanging
it out piece by piece. We do
at she finds it in her to put

e table, her fingertips brush-
the state social services can

hey mean to. They will try,
e best intentions can make
th people who love you and
heir family forever." It was

more revealing than he had meant it to be. He had a lot of respect for all the people who tried to help improve the lives of children, but respect was not the same as coming to terms with his past. Admitting that to himself made him suddenly question his own motives for... well, everything.

"Sorry for your wait, folks. But I'm here now to take care of y'all." A dead ringer for the imaginary waitress Jax had first expected to find at the Crosspoint Café appeared at the table, order pad in hand. "Just tell me what your little heart desires."

"Something I know I'll never be able to have," Jax whispered as he looked at Shelby and the baby.

"What's that you say, honey?" The redheaded waitress crinkled up her nose at him.

"He's been joking that he wants everything on the menu," Shelby chimed in, shaking her head as she looked over the specials clipped to the laminated page in her hands.

The waitress laughed. "Well, all righty then. How about I go get a couple of cups of coffee and give you more time?"

More time. That was what his heart desired. More time for Amanda and whoever had left her. *That* was what was needed. The waitress couldn't get it for Jax. But maybe he could find a way to get it for himself.

Chapter Six

It was just after 10:00 a.m. when Jax pulled the minivan into the lot next to the decades-old social services building just behind the county courthouse in Westmoreland. He had to cruise through the lot twice to find a spot, and when he did, it was in a far corner. He pulled into the spot, but his hand hovered over the key before the finality of shutting the engine off. It was only a slight hesitation, but it was all he would allow himself.

He looked at Shelby as if to ask, "Are you sure we don't just want to take her back to Sunnyside?"

Shelby heaved a resigned sigh.

The brake creaked as he set it just before he tugged out the key. Jax moved swiftly from that point on, getting Amanda out and carrying her up the outside steps and through the halls cluttered with people in various stages of getting or giving assistance.

"So much need," Shelby whispered. "Doesn't it make you wish you could do something to help?"

"I do…" Jax cut his words short. He had meant to

say, *I do what I can,* but that was no longer true. In the police force, he had served others each and every day, no matter what their circumstances were. If he took a job doing security for a wealthy community in Miami, would he still feel that same sense of service?

Before he could concoct an answer he could live with, they crossed the threshold into a waiting room outside an office. In a flash, Jax felt nine years old again. It was as if his mom had just died weeks ago, and no family member could take him in. He was just an unwanted kid with nowhere else to go.

A knot twisted low in his gut. He clenched his teeth to force himself not to go there. He tightened his grip on the handle of the baby carrier. Amanda's situation was not the same as his. Her fate would be so much better.

Please, he prayed silently as he looked at the face of the child who had come so unexpectedly into his life. *Please give Amanda a life full of love and hope.*

"Jax?" Shelby put her hand on his arm.

It surprised him, and he roused from the intensity of the moment to find those blue eyes riveted on him. Even with his heart in turmoil, Shelby's presence made him smile.

"I was saying a prayer for Amanda's future," he confessed quietly.

Her hand closed on his forearm. She smiled, but her eyes remained somber. "I've been doing that all morning."

Always a man of action, Jax used that shared concern to act as an advocate on Amanda's behalf. "Shelby, it

t sure this is the right thing
ould—"
er-haired woman wearing a
ile appeared in the doorway
follow her.
erly even. Jax tried to focus
asked Shelby questions and
, entering data into a com-
nk about was how it felt to
a big chair, hearing second-
his family wasn't ever com-

anda, sleeping soundly in her
memory of this day, but one
e to grips with the reality of
ith it for the rest of her life.
iny fist opened and closed,
eel those tiny fingers closing
dn't help all those people in
served the people as a police
mething for this little baby.
a his head when the social
Shelby about the overload
ey had all had to make. He
ck assessments as the state
e dearth of foster homes able

hild abandonment case my-
nterjecting into the middle
where he had no business of-
rt. "But I do know from the

other side of things that a lot of times, the state looks for a relative or a trusted person in the community to step up and care for the baby until something more can be resolved."

The social worker cocked her head and looked Jax over slowly, nodding. He didn't know if she was mulling over his conclusion or sizing him up as a former foster kid.

Shelby didn't look at him at all.

But Jax had no doubt as to her opinion of his not-so-subtle observation an hour later, when the two of them were headed out the door of the government building with a file full of paperwork in one hand and Amanda in her carrier in the other.

"Don't be mad, Shelby. It's not permanent."

"You just don't get it." Shelby stormed ahead, her feet hitting the pavement like they were in a pounding competition with her heart.

"Was I wrong? The social worker agreed it would be ideal for Amanda to remain in Sunnyside, where she was left, just in case the mother comes looking for her." He reached for the handle of the carrier to lift it from her.

"I didn't say you were wrong." Shelby deftly evaded his grasp, her gaze fixed on the minivan at the far end of the still crowded lot. "I wouldn't have agreed to it if I thought you were wrong."

"What then?" His long stride overtook her quick steps easily. This time, when he wrapped his hand around the carrier handle, Shelby had no choice but to stop in her tracks. He pulled the carrier gently toward

n't fix this unless I know

fingers around the handle,
ing go work all the way up
to her shoulder and down
ad no idea what to think of
it volunteered her to put all
non-plans, and all her life,
as also more of a non-life,
care of a whole tiny other
hen he realized that might
as he actually willing to do
do you mean? You want to
it to fix me so I won't mind

and shook his head. "There
ou, Shelby Grace."

cheeks at his bold yet sweet

why doing what's right for
up," he went on, gentleman
girlish blush. "I want to fix
ht, not just for Amanda, but

for a moment. She had no
given her track record with
ld her what she wanted to
im. She believed him with

ght of that before you vol-
's foster mom." The weight

that she felt had settled onto her shoulders rolled off as she finally expressed what had been troubling her since…well, ever since she could remember. "It's not that I don't want to do the right thing, that I wouldn't sacrifice whatever I had to for someone I love or someone in need. I'd just like to be the one to offer, not to just find it all laid on my doorstep with the expectation that softhearted Shelby will take up the slack. Does that make sense?"

His cheek twitched. He looked at the baby between them, then out toward the minivan. At last his gaze returned to her, and he nodded slowly. "You want your life to be your own."

Shelby smiled. "Actually, I'd like to think my life is the Lord's. But that doesn't mean that I don't have dreams, Jax. They may be small ones, not like you and your big job in Miami, but they're mine and I'd like the chance to follow them."

"I said I'd stick around long enough to find a temporary foster home for Amanda," he reminded her, his hand still clasping the handle, the toes of his cowboy boots just inches away from the cross-trainers she considered her best choice for travel shoes. "I never once said it would be with you."

"In Sunnyside?" Shelby used both hands to keep Amanda and the carrier in her possession. She did not whine. She did not scold. She simply stated what everyone who had ever known her knew. "Who else would it be with? Any other place you might find would just be a stop on the way to my doorstep."

"Is it so bad, really? As I recall, an hour ago you

were the girl who wanted to help all these people." He motioned to the scads of cars around them. He paused long enough for his calling her to task to sink in, then gently took the carrier, put one hand on Shelby's back and escorted her toward the minivan. "You can't help them, but then, isn't the saying that charity begins at home?"

"Home!" She stopped and put her hand to her head. The dull ache between her shoulder blades from handling the baby in her carrier crept upward to her neck and the base of her head. "I don't even have one of those."

"What do you mean?"

"Only that I have…*had* the cutest apartment over a garage in my rent bracket in all of Sunnyside." She dragged her feet the rest of the way to the minivan as the reality sank in. "Maybe the only apartment, garage or otherwise, in my rent bracket in Sunnyside. And I broke my lease on it yesterday."

"Then unbreak it." He opened the side door and began to get Amanda settled in the car seat.

"Right. Unbreak it." She looked at the minivan she had bought with such big expectations. She'd ended up saddled with it and a truck payment. Last night she had thought she had finally gotten up the courage to walk away from responsibilities that others had chosen for her. Today she had not only all those, but a whole raft of new ones, too.

Unfortunately, once something is broken—be it a heart or trust or promises—it was not easy to return it to the way it was.

* * *

The drive back was quiet. Jax drove. Amanda slept. Shelby plotted.

At least that was what he thought she was doing over in the passenger seat with her phone in her hands, her fingers flying over the screen. More than once she called up the calculator function, tapped in some numbers and then raised her head and stared off into the distance.

He wanted to offer a penny for her thoughts, but it seemed grossly undervalued given the circumstances.

"You know, Shelby, I've been thinking," he ventured as they pulled into the parking lot of the Truck Stop Inn and the Crosspoint Café, and she finally closed the calculator screen. "What if we set up a fund to help take care of Amanda? I'd be happy to pitch in what I can now, and once I'm in Miami—"

He cut his thought short as he slowed the minivan to a crawl in the lot. He had to do both to avoid running over the toes of half the town of Sunnyside.

"I think that's a great idea." Shelby waved to a group of high school girls holding up signs advertising a car wash. "Apparently you aren't the first to think of it!"

He guided the minivan through the crowd, and when they glided past the gas pumps, he rolled down his window to greet Miss Delta, who was shaking a jar full of money like a set of maracas.

"Sneak out of town for a few hours and lookie what happens!" she said with a smile.

Shelby laughed and leaned over to talk to her through Jax's window. "Did you organize all this after Tyler

ing to foster Amanda for

an that, darlin'. Nobody in
it to lend a hand if a hand
her head. "Nope. Soon as
your daddy got out his big-
n on the counter and told
pped out on giving him or
ter pay up, because every
sweet little baby."

a moment.

wheel as he replayed Shel-
s always assume what she
d to do it in her stead. He
d his mouth, not quite sure

Shelby chuckled. A smile
k her head. "And that, right
never save enough money
much less buy a truck or get
ng. Bless his big ol' heart."

kay with this?"

oftly that he more saw her
ard her.

hand on her shoulder in a

ople cheered their return
Miss Delta's hand. Shelby
e over her father's gesture.
and generosity surround-
n anything like it. And in

his new line of work, private security for the ultrarich, he would not likely see it again.

He dropped his hand away from Shelby's shoulder. Moments later, after they parked, he took the carrier holding Amanda.

"Is that her? Let us see, Shelby. Can I hold her?" people called as they pushed toward the minivan to get a peek at the baby.

Shelby turned to him. "I…uh…"

"Amanda has already had a lot of excitement today." Jax stepped up with his hand up to keep people at bay. Shelby might not need him for support, but she still needed someone to help her stand up for herself, and for Amanda. "I know most of you don't know me, but Sheriff Denby deputized me to help out with this case. That makes this baby my charge until further notice."

Shelby rushed to help him get Amanda out of her carrier. Their hands practically tangled as they unbuckled the child and removed her from the blanket. Finally, she lifted the baby out and placed her carefully with Jax. For just that instant, he, Shelby and Amanda seemed like the only people on the face of the earth.

They appeared to have a special bond that nobody could breach. It felt like a promise fulfilled. Was this what it was like to have a family?

The fact that he even asked himself that question startled Jax. He looked deeply into Shelby's blue eyes, hoping to find an answer there.

She smiled up at him tentatively before the crowd started to close in around them, cooing and laughing, oohing and aahing over the helpless human being cradled in his arms. The feeling dissipated—or maybe it expanded.

"So if y'all don't mind," he went on as he curled the baby close to his chest, "*I'll* be holding Amanda, and you can all come around and introduce yourselves—to both of us."

For the first time in his life, Jax went from being part of a family to part of a community. And he *liked* it.

Talk about sending up a red flag. Those were not emotions that he could afford. Contrary to what Miss Delta thought, Jax did not belong here. At least not for more than another day or so—however long it took to get Shelby and Amanda settled in a new place and the case on the right track.

"And if anyone has any information that might help us figure out who left this little sweetheart here last night, I'd appreciate you sharing it with me in the next twenty-four hours," he said good and loud, to be heard over all the chatter.

"Why the next twenty-four hours?" Shelby asked, standing on tiptoe and leaning against him as she reached in to slip a pacifier into Amanda's pudgy mouth.

"Because as soon as I gather as much info as I can and make sure you two have a safe place to stay, my work here will be done."

Chapter Seven

Frantic fund-raising, topped off with a chili supper at the café and countless recountings of the session with the social worker, had filled the rest of the day and evening. After inhaling a meal, Shelby had whisked the baby back to the Denby household. Everybody understood that she had definitely earned and needed a chance to rest and regroup. Jax had intended to follow, making the excuse that he wanted to discuss the case further with the sheriff, but Doc Lovey had put her foot down. No visitors.

"Our girls have had enough for one day, don't you think, Deputy?" she had asked in a drawl as big as Texas itself. It was fitting coming from a rawboned redhead who looked more suited to the role of cowgirl veterinarian than town physician.

"*Our* girls?" Jax had asked as he watched Shelby load the baby into the minivan amid a circle of friends and well-wishers.

Doc Lovey had pressed her hand to his back and had

given him a pat, explaining, "The whole town has fallen in love with that baby girl now, sweet thing. And we all laid claim to Shelby Grace when she wasn't much older than little Amanda is today. They're in our hearts now and for always, right where they belong."

"But I reckon that's a sentiment you understand, isn't it?" Miss Delta had appeared at his side and had looped her arm through his like they were good ol' pals from way back.

Jax had been gazing into the distance, trying to decide how he wanted to answer that, when something caught his eye. A Mustang with faded red paint, like the one Tyler had described as having been at the gas pumps the night Amanda was abandoned. His first instinct was to push through the crowd and try to chase it down on foot, but even as the energy to do so coiled tightly in his body, the car eased its way along and reached the exit onto the main road. He had to give up on the idea. He'd never reach the car in time, and his actions would tip off the driver that someone was watching them.

After all, this person could be the key to securing Amanda's future. At the very least, it could be this Mitch guy, someone who had hurt Shelby in the past. Either way, they seemed comfortable coming and going in the community for now, and Jax wanted to keep it that way until he got the chance to talk to them.

"Yes, ma'am," Jax said, finally answering Miss Delta's question, and with much more conviction than he had felt a few minutes earlier. "I believe I do understand, a little."

He wasn't just saying that. That small change

haunted Jax through the rest of the evening spending time with the locals.

That night he dreamt of palm trees and ocean breezes and giant babies with gold-plated pacifiers. He dreamt of chasing red cars in a minivan that couldn't quite keep up. And Shelby. Wherever his dreams took him that night, Shelby was there, Amanda in her arms.

So it seemed the most natural thing in the world for his whole mood to lighten when he spotted them in the back of Miss Delta's store, in front of the community bulletin board, bright and early the next morning.

"Good morning, beautiful!" He raised his hand in greeting as he came up to them.

"Jax! Shhhh." Shelby ripped off a phone number from an Apartment for Rent flyer, glancing around them. "It's not that I'm not flattered, but you've seen how fast gossip spreads in this town. I do not need anyone thinking there is anything between us but—"

"Amanda," he said, finishing for her, then squatting down to stroke the head of the baby happily gurgling in her carrier on the floor near Shelby's feet. "I was talking to Amanda."

"Oh." She blushed from the collar of her Texas Longhorns T-shirt to the tips of her adorable ears. Pushing her hair back from her eyes, she acted as if she suddenly found the phone number and info on the one-bedroom apartment fascinating.

"Though you are pretty easy on the eyes yourself." He stood and grinned at her. "And I don't care who knows I think so."

"Thank you, but I think you're being generous.

Maybe you didn't see the dark circles under my eyes."
She scanned the flyer again, running her finger along
the line that included the monthly cost. Without comment, she shook her head and crumpled up the phone
number. "Turns out one of *Amanda's* beauty secrets in-
volves getting plenty of exercise, mostly by screaming,
kicking and crying all night long."

"Is she okay?" Jax went down to peer into the carrier again. He placed the back of his hand to the baby's
forehead, not actually sure what he would feel if she had
a temperature, or what he would do about it.

"Doc Lovey looked her over and said she seems
fine." Shelby knelt down beside Jax. She fussed with the
small quilt cushioning the now sleeping baby. "Maybe
it's because of a change in formula or all the travel
or just being overly tired from her big day. Doc's advice was to note how often it happens, keep a journal
of feedings and so on…and to find an apartment with
very thick walls."

Jax chuckled at that.

"Right now I'd settle for an apartment I can afford."

"Well, I don't know how thick the walls are." Miss
Delta poked her head around the corner of the wall
where the notices were posted. "But I do have a place
where I think you'd be happy—and the price is right."

"Miss Delta, are you sure?" Shelby strolled through
the hallway of Miss Delta's rambling Victorian home.
"You've always been so protective of your privacy,
which is no small feat here in Sunnyside. Renting a
room to us when Amanda has sort of been adopted by

the whole town is kind of like throwing the doors open to everyone, isn't it?"

"Are you kidding, honey? I'd love for folks to think they can come over for a visit whenever they please." Miss Delta ushered them into the large kitchen. She directed Shelby to settle Amanda on the table and take a seat. "Ever since I inherited this place from my late aunt and uncle, I dreamed of filling it with a big family. But since Mr. Right never came to Sunnyside, I missed out on that for myself."

"If Mr. Right didn't show up here, why didn't you go looking for him?" Shelby got Amanda situated, then sat and took a good look around at the bright, roomy old-fashioned eat-in kitchen, which already felt like home to her. "Or for whatever it was you wanted in life?"

"Because I had what I wanted in life—people who love me, work I enjoy, a home. Fetch me some tall glasses from up there, won't you, Jax honey?" She pointed to an upper cabinet, then reached into the refrigerator and pulled out a big pitcher of iced tea. "I wanted a Mr. Right to add to my life, not to make it from me."

Was that meant as a message to Shelby? What did Miss Delta know about the plans Amanda's arrival had disrupted? Shelby shifted restlessly in her seat.

"Besides, even if Mr. Right did show up here, I suppose there was always a chance he wouldn't stick around." Miss Delta took the glasses from Jax and clunked them down on the counter. "Not everyone finds the sense of belonging in Sunnyside that I do. Wouldn't you agree, Jax?"

Jax cocked his head.

nying it. Shelby crossed her
s I appreciate this offer, I'm
with a baby for an indefinite
disruptive for you."

That's why you *should* move
disruption in my routine."

noo the man toward the re-
she smiled impishly at him
don't you think, Jax honey?"
ing that, they'd never know,
im wordlessly to the large
talking to Shelby.

house has been my sanctu-
or a moment, as if listening
ence answered her. "A place
gle person in town feels they
orders."

ix scoffed, setting the pitcher
sses without having poured

iness like mine in Sunny-
ama to everyone who walks
nan." She grabbed the pitcher
t, as if offering him a toast,
an pouring out the icy amber
ectations that like a mama, I
what they need doing."

i don't hesitate to tell them
they are running their lives,"
ext to her to relieve her of the
er tea pouring duties.

"And like most kids, even full-grown ones, they do not always listen to my wise advice." She scowled at his intrusion but did not fight his assistance.

"Oh, all right, all right. I'll take a room with you." Shelby got it. The whole stubbornness about accepting help, the hidden messages about how her life might end up like Miss Delta's—not one bit of the subtext had missed her attention. That didn't mean she couldn't still make her own decisions concerning what she did about it. "But I *am* paying rent."

"You don't have to pay me anything." Miss Delta picked up the glass of tea that Jax had just finished pouring and set it down decisively in front of Shelby. "In fact, I think you should quit the café and take care of Amanda full-time while she's with us."

"Miss Delta, as the town mama, I'm shocked you didn't hear that I already quit the café." She lifted the glass and took a sip, giving that time to sink in.

Miss Delta took a seat at the table even as she raised her finely plucked eyebrows in surprise. "I had heard a rumor, but you know that as a good Christian woman, I don't take stock in town gossip."

"You know it's not gossip when I tell you that I have been saving money since I was a teenager. I have enough to…" *To get me out of Sunnyside and into a whole new life.* Shelby thought of her savings tucked away, half in the local bank, half in her suitcase. Now that that plan had fallen by the wayside, Shelby decided she didn't want anyone in town knowing about it. It would only make for another story about how Shelby's big heart always got in the way of her big dreams.

to work and to take care of
ay you some rent. And she is
needs will be taken care of
ay rent."

a threw up her hands, then
y'all will excuse me a min-
and make sure your room is
o it."

a-scented perfume had not
ax braced both palms flat on
se over Shelby to say, "She's
oney you give her and hold it

d his face and got lost for a
is brown eyes, in the way his
o break into a grin. Her pulse
hen faster. Suddenly the fact
could notice all these things
up from her chair, trying to
al footing with him. "I'm sur-
ut about Miss Delta, though.
a few days, but already you

s she had expected he would.
like to know better."

e to know—to really know
, she would have retreated a
cross the room. But with this
ed to back down, to try to do
give in to the image of soft-
found confidence rushed out

in her voice as she added, "Even then, I bet they could surprise you."

"Yeah? People don't usually surprise me at all. The idea of someone I could never completely figure out is…" He inched close, until his face was over hers. Not quite as if about to kiss her, but as if making the promise of a kiss to come.

Shelby took in a deep breath.

The doorbell rang. Shelby jumped and pulled away from Jax so quickly, she bumped the table.

Amanda roused and began to fuss quietly.

"I know that sound. If I don't calm her down right now, she's going to work herself up into a wail." Shelby practically dove for the baby.

Jax headed down the hallway toward the front door. His footsteps stopped as the door creaked open and Sheriff Denby's voice bellowed, "So here's where everyone got to! Came into the café and Truck Stop Inn to catch up on the case with my newest deputy and ended up talking to myself!"

"About the case," Jax said, sounding not the least bit distracted by what had just happened. "Maybe you and I could have a word alone?"

"Alone? In Sunnyside?" The sheriff laughed softly over the sound of his keys jingling. "'Less you plan to accuse one Shelby of leaving that baby herself—again—or call Miss Delta a conspirator…"

Miss Delta came hurrying down the stairway to the foyer and stood with her hands on both hips right where Jax could see her. Shelby hoisted Amanda onto her shoulder and, patting the baby's back, took up a position right behind Miss Delta.

Jax shot a look straight past the older woman, targeting Shelby. His cheek twitched, and then he sighed and shook his head. "I just think not enough's been done to find that red car, the one Tyler thought belonged to Shelby's ex-boyfriend."

"You don't know what I've been up to while you were…" The older man gave the younger man a slap on the back and concluded pointedly, "Taking care of the girls here, son. I've known Mitch Warner since I had to give him his first talking to for rowdyism while he was still in middle school. I've made it known that I want a word with him. It may take him a while, but he'll give me a shout."

Jax looked at the sheriff, then at Miss Delta, then at Shelby and the baby. He clenched his jaw, then exhaled. "Okay then. Looks to me like everything that *can* be done has been done."

"The social worker said that statistically, mothers are usually reported or turn themselves in, in cases like this," Shelby offered. "So from here on out, it's just a matter of waiting, right?"

"Yup." Sheriff Andy's thinning white hair shone almost ghostly in the bright sunlight streaming in from the window of the front door. "No idea how long it might take. If you want to stick around and wait it out, Stroud, I could use an experienced deputy around here. Been looking for one I could train to run for sheriff one day, finally let me retire."

Jax shook his head. "Much as I'd like to see how all this turns out, I have a job waiting for me in Florida."

"Dream job," Shelby reminded him softly.

"What?" He homed in on her as if it were just the two of them standing there.

"When you talked about it before, you said it was your dream job," she reminded him.

"Oh, did I? Yeah. I guess." He ducked his head slightly and ran his hand through his dark hair like a cowboy who suddenly wished he had a nice wide hat brim to hide under to get out of the directness of her gaze. "Except, after the dream I had about it last night, I'm hoping I'm wrong about that."

"Well, if you're going to be hitting the road, son, I'm going to need your badge." Sheriff Andy seemed oblivious to the quiet intensity of the exchange between Jax and Shelby. He held out one beefy hand to the man.

"It was only temporary." Jax handed the badge back. "I don't even know why I pulled off at your exit that night, anyway."

"Probably because you realized there was something in Sunnyside you needed," Miss Delta offered, reaching out to give the man's arms a squeeze.

Jax frowned. Not an angry frown, but the kind a man made when he wasn't quite sure what was being said to him, or how to respond.

"She means you were hungry or tired or thirsty," Shelby explained, giving Miss Delta a warning glare not to try to make more of this than it warranted, especially on Shelby's behalf.

"Yeah, that's what I said. There was something that

you knew you couldn't get on that long, dark highway." The squeeze turned into a pat. "Something that you knew wasn't waiting for you at the end of your trip."

Jax studied Miss Delta for a moment. He did not contradict her. Or laugh at her conclusions.

Amanda drew her knees up and waved her fists, gurgling red faced against Shelby's tensed shoulder.

"Maybe you're right, Miss Delta," was all Jax said before he leaned over and gave the wriggling baby a kiss on the head. As he did, his eyes met Shelby's.

It seemed like the whole house fell silent for far too long before Sheriff Andy stepped up, lifted Amanda from Shelby's hold and said, "Didn't you get all that cantankerousness out of you last night, little one? Let Uncle Andy take you for a walk and see if we can't improve your mood."

"Hang on. I'm coming with you. We'll take her upstairs and pick out which room will be her nursery." Miss Delta swept her hand out, directing the sheriff along ahead of her. She put one foot on the bottom step, then turned to Jax. "I'd say goodbye, but I have a feeling I'm going to see *you* again. Whatever led you here? This truck stop mama does not believe you found it yet."

Jax opened his mouth to reply, but Miss Delta had whipped around and hurried up the stairs, calling out to Sheriff Andy to go to the room all the way at the end of the hall and see if he didn't think it was meant for Shelby and Amanda.

That left the pair of them standing alone in the foyer.

"I guess this is the part where I thank you for everything you've done to help me with Amanda." Shelby started to hold her hand out for a firm goodbye hand-shake. When he kept his hands stuffed in his pockets, she quickly pretended she needed to tuck a strand of hair behind her ear.

"I didn't do anything, really, except some really fancy minivan driving." He held his hands up, as if steering the van, grinned and gave her a wink.

"You looked good doing it." She laughed.

"Naw…" He feigned humility.

"You did. You *know* you did," she teased. "And you gave me a few hours of fun at Buffalo Betty's, which I hadn't had in forever. I'll always be grateful for that."

"You say it like you don't expect to have any fun again for a long time."

"Well, I do have some responsibilities," she said softly. "So I…uh…just want to say…"

Only she couldn't say it.

Jax nodded. "Me too."

"I didn't say anything," she protested.

"You didn't have to. Remember, I know what folks are thinking." He smiled, tapping his temple. He turned his back and reached for the doorknob.

Selby paused for a moment, not sure what to do next. She'd been stalling, just hoping that somehow she'd suddenly find a way to tell Jax how much his brief time in her life had meant to her. She wanted the nerve to let him know she wished they had met at a different time, under different circumstances.

If Shelby needed to tell him anything—and she wasn't exactly sure what she wanted to tell him—she had to do it now. "Or maybe you just *think* you know what people are thinking, because that means you can keep thinking instead of feeling what you don't want to be feeling."

He froze in his tracks. "I don't know how I feel about what I think you just said."

Shelby didn't even know what she'd said, and when she realized that, she broke into laughter. Jax joined in. It was the kind of laugh that people share to break the tension, sweet and a little bit silly. It created one last special moment just between them. Just what they needed to bring things to an amicable end.

"It's really been good getting to know you, Shelby Grace."

Know her? Jackson Stroud was never going to really know her. He was going to drive away and take his dream job in Miami, believing she was nothing more than what the town saw—softhearted Shelby. He'd never see the woman she so desperately longed to become. He'd never know that she had bigger dreams than being a waitress and that she had had, if only for a brief moment on a dark, momentous night, the courage to follow them. He'd never know that unless...

"Goodbye, Jackson Stroud. I'll be praying for you. Have a safe trip, and don't forget us." She went up on tiptoe and, with every ounce of her fleeting confidence, kissed him once on the lips.

And, unbeknownst to him, she slipped the note she had meant to leave on the door of the Crosspoint Café that night they met into his pocket.

"Goodbye, Shelby."

Chapter Eight

He was two full tanks of gas and an empty stomach down the road before Jax had any reason to reach into his pocket to pull out some spare change to pay for a snack at the gas station.

"Hey, Mister! You dropped something." The kid in line behind him stopped to retrieve a wrinkled piece of paper folded in quarters.

"That can't be mine. It's…" He looked closer. He recognized that paper. It was the note Shelby had had in her hand when she came to the café door, crying, on the night they found Amanda. He took it from the kid's hand. "It's not supposed to be in my pocket. Thanks for spotting that."

He glanced back at the soft drink and bag of chips in the young man's hands and told the clerk he wanted to pay for those as well as his own.

"You don't have to do that," the kid said. "It was just a piece of paper."

"You didn't have to say anything when you saw I

dropped this. And to me, it's more than just a piece of paper." Jax had no idea how much more until he got back into his truck, settled in with his snack and opened the folded page right there in the gas station parking lot.

To whom it may concern—plus a whole lot of people it doesn't concern but who will want to know about it, anyway.

Jax couldn't help but smile at Shelby's unmistakable style.

I love you all.

Jax paused and just let his eyes rest on the phrase a moment. It was so simple and yet so all-encompassing. And he did not doubt for one second that Shelby meant it. She really did love whoever she thought would end up reading this letter.

Of course she hadn't even met Jax when she wrote those words.

I love this town. But it's pretty clear that if I ever hope to make a life for myself, I can't stay here any longer. I think it's time I followed my own dreams. Don't worry about me. I've got all your love and all you've taught me coming with me, starting with these three rules:

1. Never forget that with God all things are possible.

2. Never let anyone else tell me what I "should" feel.

3. Never, ever trust a cowboy.

Jax scowled. He could actually see the brim of his cowboy hat lying on the seat beside him from the corner of his eye. His stomach clenched.

She had all but told him the first two, but the man

who thought he knew everybody's motivations had missed the third.

I mean it. No cowboys. I don't need the heartache.

"Heartache," he murmured. It was not a term he ever wanted to associate with Shelby Grace.

See, good old softhearted Shelby has learned a thing or two over the years. So don't worry about me. I'll be in touch when I find someplace to start again where I can be the person I am meant to be.

For now, I leave you with my love and prayers.

Shelby Grace Lockhart

Jax ran his fingertips over the round, careful penmanship of Shelby's name. He remembered the tears in her eyes the night she had intended to leave this for her father and friends to find. These words had cost her dearly, and she had given them to him and him alone.

It was a humbling responsibility she had given him. A gift of insight and a secret that so few people would ever have trusted with a stranger. He folded the note in half, then in half again. He reached over and pushed the button to open the truck's glove compartment, but even before the thing could spring completely open, he flicked it shut again.

Not just any stranger, he thought as he looked beyond the note to the Stetson on the seat. Jax never thought of himself as a cowboy, but he sure did look like one that night outside the café. And Shelby had found a way to trust him, eventually, in a way she trusted no one else.

Jax's actions had curtailed her attempt to leave town, to make that fresh start, but more importantly, he'd left her sleepless and emotionally vulnerable in that town,

with the cowboy who had broken Shelby's heart still
out there.

He tucked the note in his shirt pocket and started the
truck's engine. In minutes he was heading back in the
direction he had just come from, unfazed by the long
hours of driving ahead. He knew his responsibility in
Sunnyside was not done, and prayed that he wasn't too
late to be worthy of Shelby's trust.

It had taken hours for Shelby to fall asleep, but when
she had, she had slept so soundly that she didn't hear her
cell phone ring in the middle of the night. She glanced
at the "unavailable" number the next morning as she
fed Amanda a bottle.

She stifled a yawn and dismissed it out loud to Miss
Delta as the older woman headed off to work. "Usually
when I get a call with a hidden ID, it's someone trying
to sell me something. I'm not going to worry about it."

"That's smart, honey. You can't do anything about it
if you don't know who it was. They'll call again if it's
important. Especially if it was whoever left Amanda."
Miss Delta stopped to do one more check of her blond
hair and peachy lipstick in the mirror before she
snatched up her huge pink faux alligator purse, slung
it over her shoulder and hurried out the door.

A chill swept over Shelby's exhausted body. Could it
be? She hoisted the baby onto her shoulder. After only
three days, Amanda had already become part of Shelby's life and had taken a piece of her heart, and maybe a
bit of her memory, as Shelby had all but stopped think-

ing about a birth mother out there possibly wanting to make contact.

"I had sort of gotten used to the idea that you'd be with me awhile, Amanda sweetie. I want what's best for you, of course, but…I guess I was hoping *I* was what was best for you."

No sleep. No Jax. No job. And the idea taking seed in her head that Amanda's mother had her number and had used it. It was no wonder that Shelby decided she'd let somebody else make her breakfast that morning.

"If you came to get your job back, you're too late," her dad called out through the service window between the counter and the kitchen the minute Shelby walked through the doors of the Crosspoint Café.

"That fast?" Shelby hustled in and settled the baby carrier down in the first empty booth, then slid in with her back to the morning mayhem of the only breakfast joint in town. "I know it's hard times out there, but I can't believe anyone in Sunnyside would be *that* quick to grab my old job."

"Who said I hired someone from Sunnyside?" her dad shot back over the clunk of a couple of heavy plates being set down. "Order up!"

"I got it. I got it," came a familiar male voice that made Shelby sit up and twist around in the seat.

"Jax!"

Jackson Stroud lifted two plates piled high with eggs, bacon and hash browns in both hands. "Got hungry people waiting. I'll be over to take orders from you—that is, to take your order—in a minute, Miss Shelby Grace."

He was dressed in a long white bib apron, which covered his blue shirt and jeans, and his hair was a jumble of waves. The dark stubble on his face provided a contrast to the whiteness of his teeth as he flashed a broad grin at her.

Shelby's heart melted then and there. She honestly could not have imagined a single person she would have rather seen this morning than the one man who could help her figure out who had called last night and what to do about it. And he looked so adorable, too.

Once he'd set the plates down at a nearby table and asked how everything looked, he made his way to her side. Crouching beside her seat, he withdrew a pad and pencil from the pocket of his apron and finally looked right into her eyes. "What would you like, Shelby?"

To know everything is going to be all right. Then, gazing into the eyes of this man who was still here when *here* was not where his own dreams led him, Shelby sighed. Maybe everything wouldn't be all right, but this moment was right. Maybe that would be enough. "I'd like to know what you are doing here."

He chuckled softly and dropped his gaze to the floor, shaking his head. "I read your note."

"Oh." Her stomach clenched.

"And I just couldn't be another cowboy that let you down."

She whispered a thank-you, knowing that was not big enough to cover the depth of her gratitude.

He smiled, just a little, and acknowledged her thanks with a nod.

She wanted to say it again, and then again. She wanted him to know just how much it meant to have someone know the real her and still have come back to—

The reality of it all hit her just then. Jax had read her note. He was the only person who knew her secret—that she thought she would never have the life of her dreams if she stayed in the place where everyone cared about her so much. She pressed her lips together for a moment to muster her courage, then said, too quietly for anyone else to hear, "I gave that to you only because I thought I'd never see you again, and that you'd never see anyone here again. I just wanted one person to know how I felt, not how I was supposed to feel."

"I'm honored to be the first person to know that. Though *you* know how you feel, Shelby. That's something some folks never really figure out. But you?" He shook his head. His smile came slowly. He didn't just look at her; he met her gaze and they connected there. "You know who you are, girl. So I'm technically the second person who knows."

It wasn't particularly eloquently put, but it said it all. She knew who she was. "No one in my life has ever gotten that, Jax."

"Don't worry. I won't tell anyone what was in the note. I know it was a big deal that you picked me."

Shelby had picked him. Out of all the people she could have told who would have understood, she had chosen Jax.

"I'm sorry if I made a mess of your plans," he said.

"No! You didn't. You *couldn't*."

"I think I did." He shook his head. Even through the aroma of thick-cut bacon in the air, his motion brought with it the scent of fresh soap and men's aftershave. "First, by sticking my nose in the meeting with the social worker so that you ended up having to stay here to take care of Amanda, and then by leaving you before that situation was really resolved."

"No, don't feel bad about that. It was the right thing to do. Look at her." She reached into the carrier and lifted out her precious charge. "I was only fooling myself to think I could have left her in Westmoreland with strangers and taken off to follow my own bliss."

"Hi, cutie." Jax brushed his knuckle over the baby's plump cheek. "Miss me?"

Amanda's smile lit her whole small face.

Jax did not just reflect its light, but joined it with a grin that made Shelby actually laugh softly.

Amanda reached up and wrapped her hand around Jax's bent finger.

"I think she did." Jax laughed. "I think she did miss me."

She wasn't the only one, Shelby wished she had the courage to say.

Still smiling, he tugged free from Amanda's hold and stood at last. "You can tell me what you want anytime, Shelby."

"Really?" Her whole life, she had longed to have someone who actually cared what she wanted. Who would invite her to speak her mind, instead of assuming they knew what she would do or what was best for her. The idea of someone—of Jax—asking made her heartbeat skip a little.

She took a deep breath and looked up.

Jax pressed the pencil to the pad. "*Anytime* meaning hopefully real soon. I have other tables to wait on, so…"

"Oh. Yes. I…" She became so flustered, she actually picked up a menu to get some idea what to order. She stared at the laminated page and blinked, willing herself not to blush at having let herself get so sidetracked by this man who had come to mean so much to her so quickly. "I…don't…"

Jax slid the menu from between her fingers. "Why don't I surprise you?"

"Surprise?" In other words, trust him. "Okay. Sounds like fun."

"Then, fun it is." He gave her a wink and turned away.

She sighed, relieved to have a moment to regroup and refocus, get her mind off how she had gotten so far off track once again.

"Shelby?" Jax looked back at her. "I meant that."

"Oh, I know." She shifted in the bench, wondering who was watching them. "You take your fun pretty seriously."

He laughed, then leaned in. "You can always tell me what you want. I promise to listen and not decide I know what's best for you."

"Thanks, Jax."

He nodded, then straightened up and headed to the kitchen. He called out to the other patrons as he made his way through the café. "Be back with a refill as soon as I get this order in. Decaf, right? Got enough syrup there? Everything tasting okay?"

People responded with friendly ease.

Shelby shook her head at how seamlessly he fit into the fabric of the small community. Yet she couldn't help reminding herself that he had come back to finish what he'd begun, not to start a new stage in his life.

She reached over to make Amanda comfortable, saying, "He's not bad, is he? Wish I had more time to get to know him, but we both know he's going to be out of here as soon as—"

"Any guy who would walk away from you, Shelby Grace, isn't a man worth you wasting your time on."

Her whole body tensed at the intrusion of another familiar male voice. This one definitely *not* so welcome. Her mouth formed the name that she didn't have breath enough to say out loud. *Mitch Warner.*

"You should know. You walked out on her time and time again yourself, Mitch Warner." Sheriff Andy's voice carried over the sound of the café door swinging open and shut again.

Shelby didn't need anyone coming to her rescue, not even the man pledged to serve and protect the whole town. She tucked the blanket with the embroidered name protectively around Amanda, then raised her head, angling her chin up. She focused her mind on the promise that God would give her strength.

"I can handle this, Sheriff Andy." She threw back her shoulders and aimed a cool look at the man with the reddish-brown hair in the beat-up straw cowboy hat. "What are you doing here, Mitch?"

"I don't know what you think you *have,* Shelby Grace, but Mitch is here because I asked him to come round." The sheriff slid into the booth across from

Shelby and Amanda. "Seeing as we have an eyewitness putting his car here on the night of the baby being abandoned, I thought he and I needed to have a little chat."

"Eyewitness to *what?* What night are you talking about? You didn't say anything about—" Mitch had started to make himself cozy by settling in beside Shelby, but now he stood again. "Wait! Did you say baby?"

"Mitch Warner, meet Amanda." Shelby scooted away from the carrier, to make it easier to see the baby and harder for Mitch to share the seat with her.

"Shelby? Denby? Who's this?" Jax set a platter down on the table in front of Shelby.

"Shelby says her name is Amanda," Mitch said with a shrug. "Who are you?"

Jax started to say something, which Shelby suspected was a little more abrupt than introducing himself and giving Mitch a warm "How d'y'do?" but she beat him to it. "Mitch, this is Jackson Stroud. Jax, this is Mitchell Warner."

The two stared each other down, neither offering a hand to shake or an inch of ground.

"Now that those introductions are behind us, what I want to know is—who is *this?*" Shelby indicated the stack of pancakes with blueberries for the eyes, a strawberry for the nose, raisins for the smile and a cowboy hat with a lengthwise slice of banana for the brim and whipped cream for the top.

"I thought I'd give you a cowboy to make you smile for a change." Jax grinned at her, then gave Mitch a cold-eyed glare. "You're in charge. Go on. Take a bite out of him."

Shelby couldn't help but laugh. "Thanks."

"For a change? What's that supposed to mean?" Mitch tipped his beat-up straw hat back on his head.

"It means we've got some questions for you…cowboy." Jax stepped toward Mitch, crossing his arms over his broad chest. "Starting with why someone spotted your car around here the night the baby was left here."

Mitch did not back down. "First off, I don't owe any explanations to a waiter. Second, I ain't been around the Crosspoint since Shelby and I decided to not see so much of each other."

"Not to see *so much* of each other? You were sneaking around with two other women! The last six months of our so-called relationship, I barely saw you at all." Shelby looked down at the pancake cowboy Jax had concocted to remind her that she didn't have to settle for heartache from anyone.

You know who you are. You know what you feel.

Jax's conclusions, mixed with her own outrage, spurred Shelby to speak her mind to Mitch at last. "Mitch Warner, you are a cheater and a liar. Somebody left this precious, precious baby on my doorstep a few nights ago, and someone else reported seeing your flashy red car out by the—"

"Hold on there. Red car? Did you say *red* car?" Mitch snorted, shook his head and slapped his grubby jeans.

"Flashy? Did you call that sun-faded, rusted, bumpered Mustang flashy?" Jax asked.

Shelby whipped her head around to respond to the

man who loved jumping to conclusions about people and thinking he knew all about them. Clearly this was his way of saying he thought her feelings for Mitch had blinded her to the truth about him, and his junker of a car.

"I don't even *have* that car anymore, Shelby Grace." Mitch tipped his hat back down, casual as could be, and laughed. "Couldn't have been me over here that night."

"So you deny you own the car but not that you're a cheat and a liar." Jax folded his arms over his broad chest. "Interesting."

Shelby, who had just settled the baby back down in her carrier, inched toward the outer edge of the booth. "Jax, this isn't your—"

"Ain't you got tables to wait on?" Mitch sneered, tugging his hat even farther down over his eyes.

"Take a look around, pal." Jax stepped closer still. "They are all way more into what's going on at *this* table than at their own."

"Nicely observed." Sheriff Andy slipped from the seat and stood, clearly ready to intervene. "But I think you both need to consider Shelby's feelings and keep this to a low roar."

Both Jax and Mitch turned to the sheriff and started to speak.

"Stop it. Stop it, all of you. I don't need anyone to consider how I feel, because nobody here has ever stopped to *ask* me how I feel." Shelby bolted up from her own seat so fast that she bumped the table, the platter and the silverware, all of which clanked and clattered.

Amanda started in her carrier.

Shelby held her breath.

Mitch scowled.

Sheriff Andy and the whole café seemed to take a collective breath and hold it.

Jax leaned over to take a look.

A fraction of a second of quiet greeted them; then Amanda let loose with a wail.

"I'll take her, if you want." Jax held out his hands for the crying child. "You can handle this."

With his encouragement barely out of his mouth, Shelby reached for the baby and handed her over to the man in the busboy's apron. She *could* handle Mitch. And Amanda. And the prying eyes of everyone in Sunnyside. But knowing she didn't have to, at least not today, felt so very nice.

Jax curled the baby into the protection of his strong arms, and the infant immediately started to quiet down. Bouncing the baby gently, he turned to walk away with her, then looked back at Shelby. "I think you have a cowboy to take a bite out of."

Shelby decided not to answer that.

"Bring me a coffee, will ya?" Mitch called out.

"Not until you settle up what you owe from the last time you were in here and the time before that." Shelby's father, Harmon, marched up to the table and slapped a bundle of receipts down.

"I, uh, I'd have to run to the bank first." Mitch felt around his pockets, as if that proved he had every intention of paying. "I loaned a friend my last twenty last night and, uh…"

"Why don't I pay those in exchange for a few answers from you, Mitch?" Shelby pulled her wallet out of her purse and handed her debit card to her father.

Her father protested the idea, as did Sheriff Andy, until she reasoned with them. "Did you ever think if Mitch paid off his bill here and told us everything he knows, then you can ban him from coming back? He'll have no excuse to come around anymore."

A few minutes later Shelby had signed the receipts where her dad had run the tabs as a credit card. Mitch tucked the receipts in his pocket as proof he didn't owe anything, and explained that his red car had been in the shop for two weeks, and he had been borrowing friends' cars until he could get his Mustang back.

The car story satisfied Sheriff Andy, who headed off to his office, grumbling about being too old for all this.

Shelby couldn't shake her reservations about the whole situation.

"Thanks for paying off my debt, Shelby Grace." Mitch stood at the door of the café and patted the receipts in his pocket. "Let's get together sometime soon. I know I disappointed you, but maybe we can still be friends?"

From the kitchen she heard the sound of her father and Jax cooing over Amanda.

"You said it yourself, he ain't going to hang around Sunnyside forever. When he's gone, you'll wish you had someone to count on." Mitch waited until she turned back to him again to add, "I've changed, Shelby. I honestly think I could be a one-woman man, with the right woman."

"Thanks, Mitch," she said softly. "I hope that's true, but that one woman isn't going to be me."

She doubted that Mitch could have changed as much as he claimed, but wasn't that the nature of her own faith? Wasn't trusting people part of who she was?

She watched the man she had once hoped would help her build a real life saunter out the door.

"You okay?" Jax put his hand on her shoulder.

She turned with her arms open, wanting more than anything to get a great big cuddle. "Oh! Where's Amanda?"

"Harmon's got her."

"Harmon? You mean…my dad?" They'd met twice, and Jax was already on a first-name basis with her father? Her father, who absolutely *hated* his first name and made almost everyone but Miss Delta call him Lockhart.

"Don't worry. He knows a thing or two about baby girls," Jax assured her. "Why don't you sit down and eat your breakfast?"

She glanced back at the pancake. The fruit had slipped; the whipped cream had gone all watery. Shelby sighed. "Actually, I'm not hungry anymore."

"Then what are you going to do today?"

"Maybe I'll go back to Westmoreland. I'd like to do some shopping for Amanda." She fought the urge to yawn and lost. "Or maybe I'll see if I can't sneak in a nap."

"You shouldn't drive that tired. If you wait until my shift is over at two, I'll take you."

"I don't want you to go to any trouble." As soon as

she said it, she realized she didn't mean it. After watching Jax leave last night and encountering Mitch today, and knowing Jax would leave again in time, she wanted him to go to as much trouble as he was willing to. She wanted to have this little space of time when this one person who "got" her would go to great lengths to show her that she was worth his time and effort.

"It's not imposing." He scooped up the platter with the sad, droopy cowboy breakfast on it and guided her around in a circle so that she faced the door between the café and Miss Delta's. "The breakfast rush is winding down. Go ask Miss Delta if you can crash in one of the rooms at the Truck Stop Inn."

"But Amanda…"

"Has about half a dozen babysitters right here." He motioned with the platter toward the customers, who didn't even pretend not to be listening in. A couple even waved at her as if to volunteer for duty. "Let someone else be the soft touch for a few hours, Shelby."

She laughed. "I think you are anything but a soft touch, Jackson Stroud."

"Then you know how much I really want to do this for you." He urged her forward, set the platter on the counter, put his hands on her shoulders. "Let me. Please?"

He wasn't asking her to let him be a soft touch. He was asking her to show she trusted him.

She pressed her lips together. Before she could say anything, Amanda began to cry in the kitchen.

Her father tried to calm the child, to no avail.

her here with you guys. You
rted for the kitchen.
arm. "Shelby, we're big boys.

o be the one to care for her
helby moved his hands away,
s she slid her fingers along
a lot of time with her. You, of
ate how that makes me feel."
then cleared his throat and
still on for that shopping trip

lled as she went to collect
out how to get some rest and

Chapter Nine

Shelby came bursting through the swinging doors of the Crosspoint Café with a bounce in her step and a swing in her ponytail. "Doc Lovey has been watching Amanda for a few hours while I caught up on sleep, and she says she won't mind doing it a few hours more. In fact, she and Sheriff Andy said they'd be insulted if I came back before supper time."

Jax set the gray plastic tub in his hands on the table crowded with dishes next to him. He glanced at the clock to find that his shift had ended fifteen minutes earlier. Except for a time when he couldn't get a debit card to go through the system and the customer had gotten agitated with him, his day had gone quickly and smoothly.

He stole a peek into the kitchen through the server's window to find Shelby's father joking it up with the waitress who was supposed to be on duty now. Harmon Lockhart didn't seem the least bit inclined to remind Jax his work was done, and Jax couldn't help wondering

y

lowed Shelby to keep
y his time visiting or

is big apron, ready to
r he could do to help

, her face bright. "That
o—"
apron string wrapped
d pulled. Normally he
ut after a shift taking
ng away other people's
for a bite himself, his
d and muttered under

y figured out why they
es this a busboy." He
ead back and shut his
ay, you feel like you've

soft and swift toward

he lilt of laughter col-

er for her lack of sym-
r him, her face inches

ped and pulled away.
you doing?" Not only
aned toward her, clos-

ing the distance between them again. "You were going to kiss me on the forehead to make it all better, weren't you?"

"No. No. I was just going to…" She stepped back. She tilted her head to one side, openly considering what he'd said. When she spoke, there was a soft mix of humility, humor and awe in her hushed tone. "Yes. I was going to kiss you on the forehead and make it all better."

The emotion in her voice touched Jax. And, like most interactions in life, made him wonder at the motivation behind it. Embarrassment at having been caught and called out? Confusion over the level of trust and connection the gesture implied toward him? Or concern that after only twenty-four hours as a child's caregiver, her maternal impulses had already taken such a strong hold?

Her expression did not give her away. This woman, with trust issues and a need to please so strong that she had to write a note to say goodbye rather than confront her own father, certainly wasn't going to admit out loud what was going on in her head.

So Jax let it be. Which was not like him, either. He and Shelby had already begun to change their own patterns for one another. The realization gave him a twinge between his shoulder blades, but he didn't have time to chew on the bit of insight. He stretched his aching legs and threw out his arms to try to work loose that tightening in his back. "Okay. Let me get a cup of coffee—correction, make that let me get my fourth cup of coffee today—and we'll go shopping for baby goods."

"Four cups? Of coffee from the Crosspoint Café? I

think that's above the legal limit." She laughed. "Please, don't do that to yourself on my account."

He narrowed his eyes at her.

"I mean, on *Amanda's* account," she added, rushing to correct herself. "That is, people have been stopping by all day to bring things. A loaner crib, some clothes, a stroller. We can easily get by a day or so or until…"

"Until we find her mother?" he asked.

"I was going to say, 'Until you can go with me,' you being the closest thing I have to a baby whisperer and all," she teased.

"Me? Baby whisperer?" A few days ago he would have railed against the term. So maybe it was the exhaustion talking when he said, "I like it."

"Whether we find who abandoned Amanda or not, I still need to get some things for her. First, she's with me legally until the authorities say otherwise. Finding the person who left her won't change that."

"The person who left her?" He finally got the apron off and tossed it over the end of the counter. "You can't bring yourself to say 'mother'?"

"Just being precise," she argued.

"I know. With anyone else, I'd wonder if you had a sneaking suspicion you know who left her." He rolled his sleeves down, never taking his eyes off Shelby's face. "Like maybe that Mitch character."

"He has been driving a different car." Shelby didn't mean to sound like she was defending her ex, but she had to admit it came out that way.

Jax must have heard the hesitation in her voice. He held firm by the kitchen door and prompted, "But?"

Shelby sighed and confessed the thought whirling around in her brain all afternoon. "If there were any person on the planet I'd think would seek me out to leave his responsibilities on my doorstep, I'd pick Mitch first."

And her own dad second—not to leave a child but to dump his responsibilities on her.

Jax put his hand on her shoulder, partly to support her emotionally, partly to support himself physically, and called out, "Hey, y'all. My shift is over. I am out of here."

Before Shelby's father or the middle-aged mom picking up a few shifts as the café's afternoon waitress could reply, Jax draped his arm around Shelby's shoulders and guided her to the door. "So, a couple hours without the baby? What is there to do in this town with my feet up and my guard down?"

"Guard down?" she asked, shading her eyes with one hand as they stepped into the afternoon sun.

"After a day listening for clues, observing every detail of everyone who came into the place, I'd like to go someplace where no one could possibly be Amanda's, um, the person who left Amanda."

Shelby sank her teeth into her lower lip as she eyed her dad's pickup truck. "How are you at ranching?"

"I may be a city kid, but even I know you can't do much ranch work with your feet up," Jax said as the minivan went bumping along a pitted old road. He had offered to take his truck, but Shelby had insisted he rest and relax.

"You can if those feet are in the stirrups of a saddle."

Shelby guided the minivan down a long, dusty driveway and through an iron fence with the gate hanging open.

"Saddle?" He braced one arm against the dash as he scanned the property that spilled out before them. *Spilled* was the best way to describe it. An old trailer, some faded lawn furniture and a simple barn with a tin roof lay in front of them, looking like a child had left a handful of broken toys strewn under a cluster of small trees. He searched for any signs of life. "Like on a horse?"

"Yes. On a horse." She got out of the minivan and met him in front of it. "I thought you were a cowboy, cowboy. Don't tell me you don't know how to ride."

"I grew up in foster care in Dallas." He followed her to the barn, which looked better-kept than the trailer bearing the name Harmon Lockhart on the mailbox. "I wear a cowboy hat because I got used to wearing a hat as part of my uniform."

"In other words, you can't ride." She shook her head and motioned for him to follow her inside the barn.

"I *can* ride." He eyed the three horses in their stalls. One of them snorted and stamped its foot. "I just don't, usually."

"Well, consider this a most unusual day," she said with a laugh in her voice and a playful smile on her pretty face.

He hung back to get the best view of her moving through the barn. Sunlight streamed through gaps in the wood, creating shafts of golden light. As she moved along and disturbed the straw beneath her feet, tiny flecks of dust rose up and sparkled around her. Jax liked the effect. He liked it very much.

"Would it be rude of me to note that you are a lot sweeter when you've caught up on your sleep?"

She didn't answer, probably because she had fixed all her strength and concentration on wrestling a large black leather saddle from its resting place and onto the complacent roan standing in its stall, munching on hay.

Jax rushed to her aid.

"I've done this thousands of times before, Jax." She tried to wrench the heavy saddle from his grasp. "I can handle it."

"I know you can, Shelby." He could have easily lifted her burden, but he knew she would resent having it taken from her. He needed to help her surrender it instead. So he leaned in close, so close he could see every lash framing those expressive blue eyes, and said softly, "You can do anything you put your mind to, including letting me help you now. Because in a few days I'll be gone and wondering if there was anything more I could have done to make your life easier. Even if only for a few minutes."

"Okay," she whispered. "Help all you want."

He tried to take the saddle.

Shelby's hands clung to it, drawing her in his direction right along with it.

"Shelby…"

She was so close now, her hair fell across her shoulder and onto his sleeve. "Hmm?"

"If you want me to help, you have to let go."

"Oh!" She released the saddle and stepped back. "You put the saddles on. I'll cinch."

He did as he was told, and she dove into her end of the deal. Jax watched her fingers practically fly through the process of securing the cinch. She was something. Feisty, but not so much that she ran roughshod over others' feelings. Serious about whatever she put her mind to, but with a heart full of fun and hope.

Jax just couldn't…

The horse stamped its foot, and Shelby dodged out of the way. Jax came back to the moment. What he *couldn't* do was stand here and think about Shelby. There was no future in that. So he decided to ask about the past—the immediate past.

"So, what did you do on your first day of leisure?"

"Leisure? Taking care of a baby is not for sissies, buddy."

"I meant your first day not working at the café." Jax laughed. "Besides, I thought you were an old hand with kids."

"Old?" She made the final tug on the cinch. The horse shifted its weight. She patted its side to calm it then put on the horse's bridle.

"Experienced," he corrected, running his hand along the horse's rippling neck muscles.

"Where'd you get that idea?"

"Before I even laid eyes on you, Tyler told me that you taught Sunday school to every kid in town. It seemed like everyone I waited on today either had you as a teacher or their child does now."

She conceded his point with a shrug and a shake of her head. "They can't get anyone else to do it."

"That's not why you do it any more than that's why the sheriff stays on year after year." He followed her to the next stall, watched her arrange the saddle blanket then lifted the saddle and settled it on the back of a brown gelding. "You do it because you love it."

She caught the cinch between her fingers, placed one hand on the flank of the waiting animal, paused, then said, "No, I do it because I love *them*."

Once again he'd missed her motivation, seeing only his own. "Helping people has always been *my* goal."

She tightened the cinch. "How is that different from what I just said?"

"I didn't give much thought to caring about the people I helped." He brushed his hand along the horse's neck, not sure if it was the serenity of the darkened barn, the comfort of the calmly waiting animals or just the nearness of Shelby that got the truth out of him so easily. He shifted his boots in the straw but did not stop himself from admitting, "I did it because it made me feel important, because I thought no one else would, because—"

"Because no one helped you when you needed it." She straightened up and put her hand on his. "We often do things to heal the hurts we feel in life by trying to put them right in other relationships."

"Really? You're going to try to sell that idea to *me?* The guy who prides himself on knowing why people do what they do?" He chuckled, not because he felt insulted, but because he found her attempt to figure him out endearing.

"Oh, Jax."

"What?" He realized she had not moved her hand from his.

She didn't say another word. She didn't have to.

"You got me. I'm justifying my actions to myself." He didn't move his hand away from her, but fixed his attention on the paleness of her small fingers against his tanned skin. "Time and time again, people at the café told me if they were going to leave a baby with anyone, it would be you."

She slipped her hand away from his and went to work putting on the horse's bridle. "I know, because I'm a big pushover."

"Because you were the one who taught them about trust and devotion and putting the needs of those you love ahead of your own needs."

"Like I said, pushover. The kids I taught in Sunday school know that better than anyone." She held her hand up to keep him from contradicting her, guided her horse out of the stall then moved to mount it. When she got up in the saddle, she tipped her head to one side. "Wait a minute. The kids I taught in Sunday school!"

"What about them?" he asked over his shoulder as he went to mount the other horse.

"We're pretty confident it's not someone currently in town, but I taught for years and years. Some of those kids don't live in Sunnyside anymore. Jax, do you think it could be one of them?"

"Good place to start." He swung himself up into his

saddle. "Do you have records of your classes or photographs that might jar your memory?"

She nodded her head. "I'm sure I have some. Not every year, and the ones with kids old enough to have a baby probably wouldn't be digital. They'd be in photo albums, all packed up."

"You should go through your moving boxes and see if you can find them. I can help, if you want." He settled into the saddle and tested the reins to get a feel for them. "And before you tell me I'm willing to help in trying to reunite Amanda and her mom because I lost my own mom, that's not why I'm offering."

"Oh?"

She was using the "Don't say too much, and just let the other guy do the talking" technique, which Jax favored in interrogations. Smart girl. It worked. "This time I want to help because I care about the people involved."

"Is that so?" She gave him a sly smile, then clicked to her horse to get moving. "I think the people involved might feel the same way about you."

"What's that supposed to mean?"

"It's pretty simple, if you ask me." She turned her horse. Walking out the barn door, she clicked again, this time with a gentle kick, and called out behind her, "See if you can keep up."

The brown gelding took off at a fast trot, which didn't compare to the racing beat of her heart. Somewhere in her neatly boxed-up belongings, she might find the face of Amanda's mother. And a not quite cowboy who had come back to her aid once already—and might or might not care about her—was going to help her look for it. She didn't know how she felt about any of that.

Shelby looked over her shoulder to see Jax maneuver his horse around and follow after her like a real pro.

He didn't so much as lose his cool once as he rode after her, and in a minute overtook her.

She pulled gently on the reins to slow her horse to a walk. "I thought you said you couldn't ride."

"I didn't say I couldn't. I said I *didn't*." He brought his horse around and slowed it to match the pace of hers.

"You know that's not how I took it. I thought you were a man who says what he means."

"I am, but that doesn't mean I say any more than I need to."

"That's one of those kinds of things that seems like sound advice, but then you think about it a minute…" She gave him what she thought was a serious, probing look.

He laughed out loud, reaching down to stroke the mane of his mount. "So, you grew up out here?"

"We lived in a little house in town until I got through high school. My mom died the summer after I graduated, and I went off to college that fall. The end of that school year, I came back to Sunnyside to find Daddy had sold the house and spent all the proceeds to buy this place." She raised her face and let the sun warm her cheeks and the wind ruffle her hair back. "There was no more money for me to continue with my schooling."

"So you dropped out of college?" Jax asked over the steady clop-clop of hooves on heat-hardened Texas clay.

"I took a break. Or that's what I told myself I was

doing." She gripped the horn of the saddle, her face still raised into the breeze. "I got a little apartment and a job at the café."

"And you found out you liked it and thought maybe it could become your life's work," Jax said, finishing for her.

"Well…" She dragged the word out, unwilling to go so far as to agree with Jax's version of things. "I like the people, old friends and new ones coming in off the highway. I like hearing their stories, and I like the consistency of seeing them day after day. It's kind of like having a great big family."

"Family, huh? So is that how your dad got involved working there? You wanted to make it a family business?"

"Daddy? *He* had big plans for this place. He was going to rent stalls and give riding lessons. He even built a little arena for junior rodeos, the whole deal."

Jax looked around. She could practically hear him counting down the things that *weren't* there.

"Then the economy went belly-up," she explained. "And I got him a job at the café to bring in some extra cash to tide him over, saying he'd put any extra in a fund to help me buy the place. Only there never was any extra, and…"

"And he was the first cowboy to break your heart?"

The question took her breath away. When she recovered, she didn't answer directly. "You're actually a very good horseman."

"I'm a better lawman."

She knew that was his way of saying he had done

some fine detective work and had seen through her evasion. But he was not the only one capable of that. "If that's what you do best, then why are you going to Florida to be a neighborhood night watchman?"

He didn't have an answer.

Gotcha, Shelby thought. "Ready to let these ponies stretch their legs? If you think you can handle it, that is."

"I can handle it," he assured her. "And if you thought I couldn't ride, why'd you take off like that right out of the barn? Trying to ditch me?"

"Not on purpose," she said before she kicked her horse lightly in the flanks to take off. "But then, it seems like not a lot of things in my life get done on purpose, so maybe you'd better hang on and be ready for wherever we end up."

Chapter Ten

They rode for an hour or so, then brushed down the horses, fed them and headed back to town.

After that, and on top of a shift at the café, Jax was bone tired. Shelby had known he would be. Had she done it so he'd go back to his bunk and rest, instead of pushing her to go through her old photos to see if any faces sparked an idea of who might have left Amanda?

She wasn't trying to throw things off course. Not on purpose. But if they didn't get around to it, well, she wasn't going out of her way to make it happen.

Over the next two days, she found herself doing just about anything to keep the two of them—the *three* of them, since Amanda was always with them—busy. Too busy to get around to unpacking old photo albums, much less combing over them for faces.

The young woman who had been so certain a week ago about what she wanted to do now couldn't seem to make herself do anything, except care for Amanda and spend time with Jax.

Nothing else seemed to matter. The clock was ticking. Jax had to leave for Florida in two days, max. That made him work all the harder to try to make some progress on the case.

Shelby just wanted to make the most of whatever time they had together. She hadn't been the one to abandon Amanda. Whoever had done that knew what they had done, where they had left the baby and, according to Jax and Sheriff Andy, who they had left her with.

The story of the baby left at the Crosspoint Café had made the local papers, been covered by TV news in both Texas and Louisiana. They had taken the basic information to the Internet, and word had spread through social media. Sometimes it all made Shelby flinch.

Jax had concluded that whoever left Amanda had been desperate. For some reason they had done it without leaving a single clue as to their identity. What if pursuing them so aggressively was only fueling that desperation? What if it made things worse?

"I think you should make a plea." Jax had met her in the parking lot behind the café shortly after seven that morning.

"But I didn't do anything," she protested as she worked Amanda out of her car seat. "Isn't that something a criminal does?"

"Not a plea bargain. A plea." He gestured with both hands folded together. Like *that* made it any clearer. "We do a video. If we're right that whoever left Amanda wanted you to have her, that means they feel a special connection to you. They trust you."

"I guess so." She pulled Amanda close, holding the baby's cheek against her own. Amanda snuggled in tight, winding her fingers through Shelby's hair. Shelby sighed. "I mean, I *know.*"

Shelby did know. She had been fooling herself to think she'd ever be able to move forward in her life without having done every last thing possible to find that person. "What exactly are you suggesting?"

A few yards away, the café door swung open and Mitch Warner stepped outside. Shelby tensed. She made a quick search of the lot and spotted the familiar red car that Mitch had driven for years.

"So you make a pitch, this plea." Jax kept right on speaking, moving closer to Shelby and Amanda as if sheltering them. "You assure the person who left the baby that they are not in trouble. They need to come forward. It's what's best for Amanda."

"I don't know if I can do that, Jax," she said softly, crossing the lot until they reached the steps.

"Speak from your heart, Shelby." Jax stepped in front of her and put his hands on her shoulders. "It will be on every TV in the area by the late-night news."

"*What* will be on every TV in the area?" Mitch asked in a hard tone as he came down the front steps of the café toward them.

"I know you're right, Jax. I know I should jump at the idea, but I'm not sure it's the right thing to do. Let me think about it." Shelby stepped around him to find her ex-boyfriend standing before her. She wound her way around him, as well. "I thought you said you didn't drive that red car anymore, Mitch."

"I don't. That's not my car."

Shelby spun around and looked at Jax.

He nodded. "You take the baby inside and ask around to see if anyone knows who owns that car. I'll go get the license number."

"Let me help, Shelby. I'm not that same guy you couldn't count on." Mitch wrapped his arm around Shelby's shoulder, his hand patting the baby's head. "I can help you and Miranda."

"Her name is Amanda." Jax brushed the other man's arm away. "And we don't need your help."

Shelby sighed. "Jax, he's only trying to—"

"Hey! Hey! Don't you get in that red car and drive away from this town for parts unknown!" Mitch's arm swung from Shelby's shoulder to wave wildly as he hurried down the step toward the lot. "People here want to talk to you about you-know-what!"

Jax and Shelby twisted around in time to see the brake lights of the red car flash and the vehicle tear out of the lot, headed toward the highway.

"Why did you do that?" Jax bunched Mitch's T-shirt in one hand as he pulled the other man nose to nose with him. Actually, given how much taller Jax was, nose to chin.

"I was trying to help. I told you I've changed, Shelby." Mitch held out his hand to her. "While this guy was ordering you around, I heard that car engine start up and had to help."

"*That's* what you call helping?" Jax asked.

"Jax! Back off." The stress of thinking that someone who might have their only clue to who had left Amanda was skulking around Sunnyside, popping up right at the Crosspoint, put an edge in Shelby's tone. "He was doing his best."

"You're taking his side?" Jax gestured toward Mitch. "You believe his story that he's changed?"

"I don't know what I believe anymore." She cradled Amanda in one arm and pressed her fingertips to her temple, trying to make herself focus.

Was she angry that they'd lost the witness, or that the witness could appear at any time and threaten her growing relationship with Amanda? She didn't want to believe the worst, but she couldn't help questioning her own heart in all this. She took a deep breath, knowing she needed to spend some time in prayer over it all.

In the meantime, she put her hand up to try to get things under control again. "Getting angry with someone who is trying to help isn't, well, helpful."

Before Jax could say more, which Shelby knew would make Mitch say more, which Shelby felt sure would only confuse her more, the door of the café swung open.

"My day off, Harmon." Jax stepped back and raised his hands the way a kid might as he said, "Not it."

"It's cool, Jax man." Harmon Lockhart mirrored Jax's gesture. Laughing, he turned to her. "I thought I saw your van in the lot. Then you didn't make it inside. There's my girl!"

Shelby's tension eased at the sight of her dad's broad smile and open arms. She stepped toward him.

He reached out and lifted the baby from her arms, instantly going into full-on baby delighting mode, making silly noises and faces.

Amanda cooed and laughed and tangled her tiny hand in his faded blond ponytail.

They might have fought and fussed over the years over everything from his lack of financial responsibility to how fast he expected her to get the orders out at the café, but Shelby loved her dad. Loved him so much that when she had wanted to leave, she could not tell him to his face, because she knew it would break both their hearts. Amanda's arrival had been the push she needed to stand up to him, quit her job and tell him he had to pay his own bills. Things between them had improved remarkably since then.

"Funny, I thought *I* was your girl, Daddy." Shelby went up on tiptoe to give her dad a kiss on his tanned cheek.

"You will *always* be my girl, Shelby Grace." He gave Shelby a kiss on the cheek in return, then made a goofy face for Amanda's enjoyment. "I may not have always proved it to you. I may not have always been the best dad in the world, but who knew how much I'd take to being a grandpa?"

"Foster grandpa," she said pointedly. She needed to remind herself as much as her father of their precarious status.

"Grandpa is grandpa," Harmon shot back. "Y'all come to spend the day with me? Breakfast rush is over. My shift'll be done before you know it."

"I'm just here because I saw Shelby pull in while I was standing near the window in Miss Delta's, trying to get a good cell signal." Jax narrowed his eyes and fixed them on Shelby, saying softly, "Playing phone tag with my new boss for a couple days. I get the feeling he's getting restless."

Why Shelby found that news unsettling, she didn't want to think about. Instead she turned to her father. "I guess we've spoiled you by coming by for breakfast every morning."

"Gotten to be a pattern, all right." Her dad's face lit as if he had suddenly remembered something. He reached into his pocket and pulled out a gleaming blue plastic card. "Fact, so much I guess you left this here one of them times."

"My debit card?" Shelby couldn't remember when she had used it at the café. Or when she had used it at all. She'd been relying on the stash of cash she'd taken out of savings when she expected to leave town. People all over town had donated the things she needed for Amanda's care. "Wow. I don't think I've used it since… Did I use it the day you were here, Mitch?" she said, turning around to look at her ex. "Mitch?"

"He took off toward Miss Delta's after your dad came out," Jax told her.

Shelby sighed. She wanted to believe Mitch had changed. She really did think he was trying. But it was so typical of that man to have headed off the minute the conversation wasn't centered on him or something of interest to him.

"I've got to get back to work." Shelby's father gave her another kiss, this time on her temple. "I'm taking my girl inside to show her off some. You ought to be more careful with your bank card, Shelby Grace."

"Did your dad just try to school you on money matters?" Jax grinned at her.

"Mitch trying to be helpful. Dad being smarter about

finances than I obviously have been. It's a world turned upside down, I tell ya." She met his gaze, and her heart leapt.

"I don't know whether to help you set it right again or to tell you to hang on and enjoy the ride."

He had said exactly the right thing. Exactly what she had been feeling. Shelby smiled. She wondered if, after the arrival of Amanda and the impending departure of Jackson Stroud, her world would ever be the way it once was. "I vote for enjoy the ride...while it lasts."

"Okay then." He gave her a nod. "Where shall we start?"

She looked at the card in her hand, then at the doorway through which her father had taken Amanda into a world of kindness and love like the baby had probably never known. They had found the baby with absolutely nothing and had given her everything when they gave her a home and love. But they couldn't promise her those things forever.

"Start?" Shelby shook her head, then laughed. "I have a great idea. Let's go shopping!"

Jax stood at the end of the long hallway in the mall in Westmoreland, waiting for Shelby to return from changing Amanda's diaper. His fingers brushed the edge of the slim phone in his pocket. He could probably get a full signal here if he wanted to call his future boss and check in.

"*If,*" he muttered to himself, staring at his inverted image in the curved chrome top of a nearby trash can. He couldn't help thinking of Shelby, marveling at how her world seemed turned upside down. He knew exactly how she felt.

And he didn't like it. The night he pulled off the highway to grab a bite to eat at the Crosspoint Café, his life had been set. He had had plans. He had had a direction. He had…

"Everything is taken care of!" Shelby came striding down the hall, Amanda grinning in her arms.

He'd had nothing. And he had *liked* that. Nothing to hold him back or weigh him down. Nothing to stand in his way. Nothing to set his world on its head, so no reason to care if it ever got set right.

Shelby and Amanda reached his side, and his gaze lifted from his own image to the reflection of the three of them in the large plate-glass shop window across from them. In an instant, the world looked righted again.

"Let's start at the baby shop over there." Shelby pointed, and Jax put his hand on her back to allow her to step in front of him and lead the way. To everyone around them, he knew, they seemed a happy family. Shelby the perfect mom and wife, he the loving husband and doting daddy.

Those were not terms he ever thought anyone would ever apply to him, even mistakenly. The baby held her arms out to him, and he took her without a moment's hesitation.

"Okay, you kept the conversation on all the things you wanted to look at for Amanda the whole drive here." "And off the topic of making that plea or going over your old photographs," he chose not to add. "But can you tell me *why* you feel you need all that stuff? I mean, you've had tons of donations from people all over town."

"I know, and it's been amazing, the outpouring of

support." She stepped inside the store filled with cribs and furniture and clothing and took a deep breath, as if inhaling the scent of the pastel candy colors everywhere—yellow, green, purple and, of course, pink and blue. "But most of those things were hand-me-downs. Bought with someone else in mind and easily cast off."

"Some people would call that recycling. Good stewardship, you know."

"You're right. I get that. A waitress at the Crosspoint doesn't save enough to give herself a fresh start in life without knowing a thing or two about good stewardship." She stopped to look over a display of the tiniest shoes Jax had ever seen. She plucked up a pair that looked like satin ballet slippers and showed them to him, her eyes practically sparkling. "What do you think?"

"Personally, I prefer a good pair of boots."

"I don't mean for you."

"I don't, either." He spun the display around half a turn and picked up a pair of pink and silver cowgirl boots no bigger than the tiny slippers in Shelby's hands.

"Maybe we'll get both." She laughed. "Who knows, maybe her grandpa, um, *foster* grandpa, will finally get to work on that dream ranch and have her riding before she can walk."

"Shelby…"

"But they are both precious and just perfect for you, Amanda." She gave the child a kiss on her chubby hand. "No matter what, right?"

"Shelby, you know it might not work out that you have her long enough to see her ride a horse, much less take her first step."

"I know, Jax." She fidgeted with the baby's hand-me-down outfit, getting it just so before she looked up into his eyes. "Why do you think I wanted to come shopping for her today?"

He had no idea. That's right—Jackson Stroud, who prided himself on knowing the reason behind every person's actions, had no clue about this blue-eyed waitress with a heart bigger than the state of Texas. "I asked you that question first."

"So Amanda will have some things that are hers. Not secondhand. Not bought with love for another child." Shelby's voice cracked. She clenched her jaw so tightly that when she tipped her head back to try to stay the wash of tears in her eyes, Jax could see her swallow as if to push down a lump in her throat.

He wanted to take her in his arms, kiss her head and tell her it was a good thing she was doing and not to cry.

Before he could reach for her, she moved away, touching things in the store as if they were precious treasures as she went along. "Most people have that, you know? A stuffed animal, a pair of booties, a photo, some keepsake from when they were a baby. Something that tells them, 'From the very first day God placed you in my heart, you were loved.'"

Now Jax had a lump in his throat. He thought of the blanket he had carried in his luggage from foster home to foster home and had tucked under his pillow for years, until it was nothing more than a rag. He had eventually retired it to a trunk that was now sitting in storage in Florida, waiting for him to come claim it. His mom had wrapped him in that blanket when he was a newborn, and it was all he had left of her. Even he, jaded and seemingly forsaken as he was by his later childhood, had what Shelby wanted to give Amanda.

"Okay then, let's get them both." He put the cowgirl boots on top of the ballet slippers, then glanced around. "I think we're going to need a shopping cart."

They filled up two baskets the shop provided before they moved to the checkout.

"When we're through here, I'll take this stuff to the van and we'll see what else we can find for her," Jax offered.

"Oh, what a darlin', darlin' little girl. How old is she?" the clerk asked as she began ringing up the purchases one by one.

"Almost four months," Shelby said, touching her finger to the baby's nub of a nose.

"Only *four months?* And look at you! You've already got your figure back! She's your first, I'll wager."

"Well, she's—"

"I have three. All boys. What I wouldn't give for a reason to buy one of these." The clerk peered closely at the tag on a bright pink tutu, never even noticing the discomfort in Shelby's expression as she shifted her weight and tried to explain the situation. "I tell you, I have yet to lose those last ten pounds of baby fat after my youngest was born."

"Really, I never—"

"How old is your youngest?" Jax stepped in to protect Shelby from getting emotional over having to tell Amanda's story again. If Shelby knew that was why he had done it, she'd probably have a fit, he realized.

So, he decided on the spot, if the diversion didn't work, he'd try something new. Anything to keep the tears out of those blue eyes.

"My youngest? Oh, he's nine."

"Months?" Jax asked, even as Shelby glowered at him for butting in.

"Years!" The clerk laughed and hit the total button. She announced the price, accepted Shelby's debit card and swiped it through the slot in the front of the machine. "Just put your pin number in there."

Shelby obeyed, then held out her hand to take the card back.

The clerk started to hand it over, eyes on the digital screen in front of her, then froze. "Oh, dear."

"What?" Selby leaned in to try to get a peek at what had the clerk obviously unsettled.

"Your card was denied."

"It must be a mistake. I know for a fact I have plenty of money in that account. Can we try it again?"

They did, with the same result.

"I don't understand."

"Well, it's not giving me any information on this end." The clerk frowned. "Do you think you could have reached the one-day limit on your account?"

"This is the first time I've used it in days."

"Because it was out of your hands for days." Jax hated to sound like a cop bringing up an ugly and uncomfortable possibility. "I think we better make a call to the bank."

Chapter Eleven

"**A** thousand dollars is a lot of money to me." The printout of her bank account's activity rattled in Shelby's hand. She scanned the numbers again, then again, before she finally laid it down on Sheriff Andy's desk for him to look over. Then, before he could actually do that, she began pointing out where the money had gone. "Five hundred of it since midnight last night, buying things online. That was my limit for the day."

Sheriff Andy adjusted his reading glasses, pursed his lips and finally had to snatch away the page to give it a good long look. "Looks like the thief played it smart at first. Spent a little bit here, a little there, so you wouldn't notice. Just like the others."

"Others?" Jax folded his arms.

When he first followed them into the office, lined with file cabinets and an American flag, a big metal desk and chairs, Shelby worried she'd feel overwhelmed by his nearness. Now she realized Jax would ask the questions the situation had her too frazzled to ask.

"Had three other cases of local folks reporting money missing from their accounts." Sheriff Andy flipped open a file on his desk and laid Shelby's bank statement on top of the pile of papers inside. "May be some more belonging to people just passing through that we don't even know about, and some folks may not have caught on yet."

"It's my fault. I should have known my card had gone missing." She wasn't sure whether to be angry or burst into tears.

"You've had a lot on your plate, Shelby." Sheriff Andy gave her a fatherly pat on the hand. "What with caring for Amanda and doing all you can to figure out who might have left her."

Shelby pressed her lips together. Her heart grew even heavier with the knowledge that she had tried harder to find Amanda's mother.

"Any progress on that from your end?" Jax stepped in to ask the sheriff.

"Doc Lovey has kept her ears open." He absently bent the shell of his ear forward as he studied the file before him and kept speaking. "Which, speaking strictly as her darlin' husband of thirty-six years, is an accomplishment, because she'd rather keep her mouth open, asking questions and getting to the heart of matters."

"I bet she'd say the same of you," Shelby teased.

"Me? No. I've found, like our friend Jax here, a good lawman learns as much or more from what doesn't get said as what does." The sheriff closed the file, peeled off his reading glasses and rubbed his eyes. "Pays to keep your mouth shut sometimes."

"You speaking as a husband or lawman?" Jax asked.

The sheriff laughed. "Anyway, we haven't got any credible tips or clues. You get anywhere trying to jog your memory, Shelby?"

"I just… I haven't…" She felt embarrassed at her inability to make progress. "Can we talk about this stolen money thing right now?"

"I don't know what to tell you." Sheriff Andy held his hands out to his sides. "This is our first case of something like this targeting locals, to be honest."

"We saw a lot of this kind of identity theft in Dallas." Jax moved forward and put his hand on the closed file. With a look, he seemed to ask permission to check it out.

The sheriff hesitated, then gave a gesture of consent. "If you can offer any advice, then, I'd appreciate your consult on it."

"The online purchases may be your key to tracking down the thief." Jax flipped through the pages, back and forth, then back again. "Check where the orders came from, where they were sent…"

"We did a few, much as time and manpower allowed, but in the end, whoever is doing this is using the cards all over the area and using a different computer every day. A few at libraries, one at a hospital, using Wi-Fi or no-contract cell phones in coffee shops, hotels, fast-food places."

Jax shook his head. "It may take these people months to get it all sorted out and to feel confident they won't get hit with a problem over it again."

"Worse than that." Shelby put her head in her hands.

"It makes me wonder who I can trust, even in Sunnyside."

"What do you mean?" Jax tossed the file down.

"The card was lost in the café. Doesn't that mean someone in Sunnyside must have been using it?"

"Maybe, maybe not." Jax moved around to the same side of the desk as Sheriff Andy. "You ever run a check on Mitch Warner?"

"Mitch? Jax, the man might have been a liar and a cheat, but he would never have stolen money from me." Even Shelby couldn't believe she'd used that as her best defense for the man she had been so infatuated with for far too long.

"I didn't see any reason to check on Mitch." Sheriff Andy scooted over. He clicked the mouse, and the computer screen flickered on. "You got a hunch?"

"Just see if he still has that red car registered in his name."

Jax hated leaving the sheriff's office without any solid information about Mitch Warner, but a call from the dispatcher about multiple small but urgent issues had taken precedence. So over Denby's complaints about reduced staff and aching knee joints, Jax had shuffled Shelby into the minivan and returned her to Miss Delta's house, where they'd left Harmon Lockhart watching Amanda.

"That ol' cowboy cook dad of yours does look like a natural as a grandpa," Jax said as he and Shelby sat in the parked minivan outside the house. Mostly he wanted to get Shelby's mind off her money woes. Also,

: ol' cowboy cook, and since
ould soon come to a close, he
tand that he was leaving her
' makes you want to rethink
rs, the one about never trust-

ing it all afternoon long." She
seat belt, and it retracted into

afety belt, as well.

her forehead and winced. "I
e it to read 'Never, ever trust

took her raised wrist in his
live like that."
d her arm free. "You do."

ated sigh. "Why else are you
e out people's motivations and
' So you can get ahead of what

ork," he protested.

han anymore, Jax," she said
down his arm as if offering

y to that. Or maybe he had
it that no single thought rose
as right. On all counts. And
m at his own game when she
the motivation behind the way
Ie didn't trust anyone.

Or he hadn't trusted anyone. Until Shelby. That was why he couldn't let her embrace this new attitude. He knew the lonely and bitter life it could lead to.

"Shelby Grace, I've just got to say—" The electronic notes of his ringtone cut him off. He glanced at the phone on the dash to see the Florida area code and number below the photo of the community clubhouse where his new office would be located. It was his new boss. He reached out and slid his thumb over the button to send the caller to voice mail. Eventually he was going to have to talk to the man, give him an update and a firm date of his arrival. But not just now.

"You know, I think you should be reevaluating those life rules of yours, Shelby." He reached out and took her hand. "Starting with asking yourself why you put that 'With God all things are possible' as number one."

"God I trust. It's people who are giving me a problem right now, Jax."

"Nope. Sorry. Doesn't work that way."

"You're the one who thinks Mitch is involved."

"I did not say that. I also didn't say there aren't some people out there who don't deserve your trust. But, Shelby, you've got to trust that there are plenty of good people out there." Jax fixed his gaze on the porch, where Miss Delta had settled on the arm of Harmon's rocking chair, and the pair of them were cooing to Amanda. "You are looking at two who certainly earned it, your dad and Miss Delta."

"Three," she said softly. "I see three people who have earned my trust."

"Amanda is kind of young but—"

"I'm looking at you, Jax." She leaned in and placed a kiss on his lips.

With that kiss, Jax felt his ties to Sunnyside, Texas, and Shelby beginning to slip away. He reached out to her. He touched her hair, her face, and leaned back in, unwilling to let go yet. Just one more kiss, a real kiss, a goodbye kiss before he—

A loud banging from the back of the minivan made them both jump.

Shelby gasped. She pulled away and looked around.

Jax gritted his teeth, determined not to let loose on Harmon for his idea of a joke in scaring them, only to look up and find Harmon and Miss Delta still on the porch—and Sheriff Denby's grinning face at the driver's side window.

A few minutes later, they were all sitting on the porch with ice-cold lemonade in tall tumblers in their hands.

"So, Mitch did still own that red car?" Jax asked

"He reported it stolen this morning," Denby confirmed.

"Before or after we saw him at the café?" Jax pressed the issue.

"Right after, it would seem. Got the info on it in that flurry of calls that came in while you were in my office, since the car was registered in this county."

"One cowboy. That's one cowboy who can't be trusted," Jax rushed to remind Shelby.

"Mitch Warner? A cowboy?" Harmon scoffed. "What's the saying? A cat can have kittens in the oven, but that don't make them biscuits. That boy ain't no more cowboy than…" He looked at Denby, then at Jax, and shrugged. "Than a kitten is a biscuit."

"You all think Mitch stole from me and made this up to cover for it, don't you?" Shelby shook her head.

"It's wrong to jump to conclusions." Miss Delta rushed to play the diplomat, but not a single face on the porch reflected that attitude.

"I'd sure like to ask him some hard questions." Denby took a long sip of lemonade.

Jax sat forward on the porch swing. "*Like* to? You mean you aren't going to?"

"Not 'less I can get him to come to the office, son. I don't have time to run him down. I'm operating on a skeleton staff as it is."

"I've seen your staff, Andy, honey." Miss Delta got up and gave him a brisk rub across the shoulders. "They are some of the best-fed skeletons I've ever seen."

Denby chuckled. "I would personally like the time to take up jogging and some of that exercise dancing to take the pounds off, if I could ever get my name off the ballot for sheriff."

Again Jax's phone went off. He knew better, but somehow the ring seemed more insistent this time, almost aggressive. He took a peek at the caller ID.

Shelby leaned her head next to his to ask, "A building is calling you?"

He glanced up and into those eyes. The eyes that had first touched his conscience with teary defiance now held a sadness that he could not bear. He sent the call to voice mail once again.

"I can't help you with that dancing thing. I don't even

ge of you trying it out of my
uffed his phone in his pocket.
u with Warner."

ack?" Sheriff Denby pinched
side of his glass and gave it a
uice squirting into his drink
That's a temporary fix. No
d, you wanted me to talk to
ge a political appointment to
ed his tanned, beefy hand to
juice off the boldly etched
-and-silver star.

find Warner and see what he
ead to Florida."

Chapter Twelve

"What are you doing here?" Mitch met them in the driveway of a small frame house in a neighborhood a couple of miles outside Sunnyside.

His shirtsleeves were unbuttoned, his hair a mess, and he was hopping on one booted foot while trying to pull his second boot on. He looked like he'd been sleeping or, at the very least, lying on the couch, watching TV in the middle of the day.

Shelby slipped out of the passenger side of the new temporary deputy's sleek black pickup. He'd said he didn't want to tip Mitch off that they were looking for him by being seen around town in Shelby's minivan. That rang true enough to her, but she also noted that the tall, broad-shouldered man in the low-fitting Stetson climbing out of that big black truck made an impressive—to some people, maybe even intimidating—sight.

Mitch glanced her way, then back at Jax, then back at her again. "Hey, Shelby. How'd you know where I was living now?"

Shelby winced. Mitch seemed to change his living arrangements every six to ten months, always saying he was moving up to the next good thing. Why hadn't Shelby realized he might really have just been moving away from the last bad thing?

"You filed a police report today. Gave this address." Jax strode right up to Mitch, close enough that if the shorter man lost his balance while struggling to put his boot on, he'd go face-first into Jax's chest.

"I don't know what you're here for, Stroud, but I..." Mitch forced his foot into the boot, then stomped it on the cement drive a few times to get it all the way on. When he straightened up, he squinted at Jax and spoke through clenched teeth, like a bad guy in a Western hoping to call the hero's bluff. "I reckon you're sticking your nose where it don't belong."

"Got the authority of the great state of Texas, or at least this county's sheriff's department, which says I *do* belong here." At this point, on a TV show, the deputy would flash his shiny badge to add some clout to his words. Jackson Stroud didn't need that kind of clout. "I just came to ask you a few questions."

"I didn't do nothing." Mitch turned to Shelby. He stabbed his fingers through his reddish-brown hair a few times, squashing it into place as he asked her, "You believe me, right, Shelby?"

"I want to believe you, Mitch." That summed up their relationship and probably explained why other people thought they could predict her responses and sometimes needed to push her toward the best action. She wanted so badly to think everyone was really trying to do the right thing. "You just make it hard to do."

"Because of this place?" He motioned to the house behind them. "I don't live here. I mean, my name's not on the lease. I've just been crashing with some friends until I can get on my feet."

"What friends?" Jax asked, eyeing the house.

"Uh, people." Mitch shrugged. "They come and go. It's not a formal deal, you know. They're good people, and they help each other out."

"By loaning each other cars?" Jax asked. He stepped to one side and craned his neck to check the side of the house.

"Yeah, exactly." Mitch folded his arms and anchored his boots in the middle of the drive.

The two of them gave Shelby the feeling of a storm brewing, and it made her stomach tighten.

"Then what did you do with your car, Mitch?" Jax crossed his arms, as well, fixed his eyes on the other man and narrowed them to slits. "Loan it to someone, then report it stolen to cover up for…something?"

"Yeah."

Jax shot a quick glance in Shelby's direction.

"No!" Mitch threw his hands out.

"What is it, yes or no?" Jax pressed.

"Yes, I did loan my car out but, no, that ain't the whole story. I got my car back, and this girl, Courtney, who I'd let use my car before, disappeared with it."

"So you're sticking with that story?" Jax spoke softly, without even a hint of a threat.

In fact, if Shelby had her eyes closed, she might have

thought Jax was actually accepting Mitch's story. Yet the immovability of his stance, even the hint of a smile on his otherwise calm face, gave the feeling that Mitch was about to learn firsthand why you don't mess with Texas's lawmen.

"It's true," Mitch protested.

"So you have no idea where the red car is?" Jax nodded, recounting the details. "The car that was in the parking lot this morning, when you tipped off the driver of said car to hit the road?"

"Oh, Mitch." Shelby had had as much of the man's lies as she could stand. "What have you done?"

"Listen to me, Mitch. I'm trying to help you, give you a shot at doing the right thing. Take it. Tell me what's really going on."

"Nothing, man." He held his hands up and took a step back from Jax, then turned to Shelby. "I mean it, Shelby. I'm innocent."

"Mitch Warner, I can think of a lot of words to describe you, but *innocent* is not one of them." Her head was swimming with all this information. "Stolen or not, Mitch, you knew who was driving your red car all along, even way back when Sheriff Andy first asked you about it, didn't you?"

Mitch grimaced.

Shelby's heart sank. "You wanted me to believe you had changed!"

Mitch squirmed.

"Look, I don't know you, and I don't know if you've changed or if you've always been the man I see standing here right now," Jax said, leaving no doubt that the man he saw before him did not impress him much. "I do know that there is someone out there who left a baby on a doorstep. That is an act of desperation, which tells me that person needs help. By refusing to tell us what you know, you may be keeping them from getting that help."

"I…I didn't think of it that way." Mitch peered over his shoulder, then cleared his throat.

"You have a full name to give us?" Jax maneuvered his way between Mitch and the house. "A whereabouts would be even better."

"She's got so many names, I can't remember them, and if I knew her whereabouts, then I wouldn't have reported my car stolen, would I?" Mitch took a couple of shuffling steps toward the house.

Jax shifted just enough to block Mitch from having a clear path inside. "You'd tell me, would you?"

Mitch seethed silently for a moment, then took a deep breath and let it out in a big huff, looking more like an exasperated teenager dealing with a tough teacher than a grown man facing an officer of the law. He motioned toward the front steps of the house, as if asking them to pull up a chair and get comfy. He sat down on the left side of the bottom step.

Shelby took the second step from the top, on the right side.

Jax remained standing, but with one boot on the bottom step, not far from Mitch. He looked ready for anything Mitch might say or do.

Shelby was grateful for that and for all he was trying to do for her here. She shaded her eyes to look up at him, standing so tall against the bright Texas sky, and before she knew it, she found herself smiling.

Jax nodded her way. The smile he gave her seemed to tell her not to worry, he had everything under control.

"Now, where were we?" Mitch asked, clapping his hands together, then rubbing them and grinning. "You were here to get the lowdown on finding my stolen car?"

"If that's what you have to tell yourself in order to finally give up some useful information, then sure, that's why we're here." Jax stretched his arm out and rested one hand on the iron handrail. "We needed the lowdown, so naturally we thought of you."

"I told you what I know. My buddy who owns this house met Courtney at a bar a few weeks ago." Mitch jerked his thumb over his shoulder to the small but neatly kept home. "Since then she's been around, comes and goes, borrows cars but always brings them back with gas in them, so nobody minds. That's all I know."

"She borrow your car the night Tyler said he saw it at the gas station?"

"She could have. I mean, without me knowing it. Sometimes if there are a lot of people, a person just grabs the keys and takes the last car in the drive."

"Friendly place," Jax said to Shelby, sounding far more congenial than she'd have expected him to be. He even dropped his hand, as if just about to accept Mitch's explanation. Only, he clearly had not accepted it, which made it all the more pointed when his expression went flinty, and he homed in on Mitch. "But didn't you tell Sheriff Denby your car had been in the shop at that time?"

Mitch opened his mouth, then shut it. He made a sort of halfhearted gesture with both hands. He started to speak again but stopped. Then he sighed and turned to look up the stairs. "Here's the thing, Shelby."

"Oh, no!" Shelby stood right up. "Not the old 'Here's the thing,' Mitch. When you start in with that, you might as well say, 'Let's draw a big red circle around what I'm about to tell you, because *this* is the part I want you to believe, in spite of all evidence to the contrary.'"

Jax laughed. "I'm getting a feeling that nobody is going to buy what you're peddling with that line anymore, Mitch."

If someone else had said that, they would have meant Shelby was not going to buy what Mitch had to say. They would have been letting Mitch know what they thought Shelby felt and what she was going to do. But when Jax said it, because of the way he said it and because of who he was, what Shelby heard was "Shelby's made herself crystal clear, and I agree with her."

She pulled her shoulders up. "Just tell us what you know about this Courtney, Mitch. No excuses. No long stories."

"All right! All right!" Mitch stood up, looked up the steps, then out at the driveway. "My car *was* in the shop, because Courtney took it that night, put over a hundred miles on it and somehow knocked the muffler loose. This time, she really did steal my car."

"Warner, man, your story just does not hold together." Jax shook his head. "How could she have stolen your car when you told her to drive off in it this morning?"

"What do you mean?" Mitch looked sincerely confused, maybe a little hurt, by the line of questioning. "Didn't you hear me yellin' at her *not* to take it to parts unknown?"

Jax clearly wanted to respond to that, but the look on his face said he had no idea how.

"I believe him, Jax. He may be a practiced liar, but he clearly needs that practice. Take him by surprise, and he's not so..." She looked over the disheveled man standing there, scratching behind his ear and shifting from foot to foot. "Smooth."

Jax chuckled, not laughing *at* Mitch but *with* Shelby. It was a subtle kindness and cool control that marked him as a thorough professional and a good man. It was the kindness-and-good-man part of that equation that had Shelby weak in the knees.

Jax took a deep breath and pushed his hat back on his head. He exhaled, shaking his head. "Okay, then, Mr. Smooth Guy, I'm guessing you also don't know anything about Shelby's debit card situation."

"Just what they're talking about in the café," Mitch said, tucking his hands in his back pockets.

"You mean the café this morning?" Jax asked, seeking clarification.

"Yeah. Sorry, Shelby. Tough break, huh? But the bank covers that kind of thing, right?"

"This morning, when we saw you?" Jax asked, pressing on.

"Yeah, that's what I said," Mitch snapped.

"Jax, why are you being so..."

Jax started speaking the same time she did, and when

she let her words trail off, he kept talking. "In the café this morning, when we saw you, hours before Shelby even found out about what happened with her account?"

"Yeah." Mitch did not miss a beat. "People were talking about who all had their accounts hacked around town, so when you said Shelby had a problem…I'm not stupid. I did the math."

"You know, Mitch, I believe you." Jax gave the other man a buddy boy–style smack on the back. "You have done the math."

Shelby knew that Jax had no interest in being Mitch's buddy. "What's that supposed to mean, Jax? Are you accusing Mitch of something?"

"You asking me if I'm suspicious of the guy, the answer is yes." He looked right at Mitch and did not back down. "But I'm just doing the job Sheriff Denby expected of me. Asking questions, looking for motivation."

"You want to know my motivation? It's taking care of Shelby. That ain't no lie. Look me in the eye, Stroud. You'll see it. That ain't no lie."

Jax did look Mitch in the eye, and to Shelby's surprise, her ex held that look and did not back down.

"Okay, Mitch. You want to do right by Shelby, then if you see this Courtney or if you hear from her—"

Mitch held up his hands to let Jax know he was miles ahead of him. "I'll let her know you're looking for her."

"Please don't. In fact, maybe it would be best if you didn't *do* anything. Just ask her if she was there the night Amanda was left, and if she was, if she saw anything—a car, a person, a note flying off in the wind.

Even something that doesn't seem important but got her attention. Just find that out and let us know. Got it?"

"*That* I will do." Mitch nodded at Jax, then faced Shelby, and his expression softened. "I won't let you down, Shelby."

"I believe you, Mitch." She smiled as she came down the stairs past Mitch, then past Jax, who lingered behind for just a moment.

"I believe you, too." Again Jax played the buddy card, putting his arm about Mitch's shoulder and giving a shake. Then he leaned in close and spoke low in a tone that sounded anything but friendly. "I also believe I wouldn't want to be you if you do anything that hurts Shelby or Amanda and keeps them from getting this resolved."

"What did you ever see in a mess like that Mitch?" Miss Delta didn't even let Shelby finish recounting the story of their exchange with her ex-boyfriend before she started shaking her head and tsk-tsking.

Shelby had insisted on coming straight home to Miss Delta's after that. She had missed Amanda and hadn't wanted Miss Delta to feel taken advantage of by being asked to watch her for any longer. Jax had intended to drop Shelby off and circle back to watch the house for a while, thinking this mysterious Courtney and the red Mustang might show up again once she felt the coast was clear.

However, just dropping someone off was not an option in Sunnyside. Miss Delta and the baby had been waiting on the porch for their return, and the minute he'd pulled into the drive, she had rushed up and had started asking questions. Then the offer of pie and coffee. And before he knew what hit him, Jax was seated in the bright, welcoming kitchen with a fork in his hand and the whole story on his lips.

"Mitch?" Shelby acted almost offended by the suggestion of her bad taste in men. Though the twinkle in her eye when she looked at him gave her away. "Weren't you listening? Jax was the one making the veiled threat."

"Veil? Me?" It was his turn to overplay the outrage. "I never once wore one of those in my life."

Miss Delta let out a peal of laughter.

Shelby smiled and shook her head, murmuring something to the baby in her arms about Jax's silliness. The room went quiet for a moment before Shelby seemed compelled to add, "Go ahead. Make a joke out of it all, but I'm telling you, Mitch was not lying."

"No argument from me." He took a bite of pie.

"Really?" Shelby jerked her head up from fussing over Amanda.

"Sure. Especially if you were listening." Jax lifted his coffee cup and peered into the dark, rich liquid swishing against the delicate white china. "He practically told us he would warn this so-called car thief we were on her trail."

"He's not a cop, Jax. He didn't know what he was supposed to do."

"*That* I will do." Jax poked the air with his fork, as if underlining every word for emphasis. "That's how he put it when I told him all he had to do was get us some more information."

Jax couldn't help feeling he was losing ground to a guy who had broken her heart over and over already. People who cared for Shelby didn't care for Mitch—and he had probably played a hand in the theft, or at least protected the person who had stolen a chunk of her life savings. It should have aggravated him, or at least annoyed him. Instead he found himself grinning at her and thinking, *That's my Shelby.*

His Shelby? No, Shelby was her own woman. And if he could just get her to the point where she didn't bring this Mitch character back into her life and where she had done all she could for Amanda, Jax could move on with a clear conscience. A heavy heart, but a clear conscience.

"Hey, since I'm here, why don't we go through those photo albums?" He set the fork down on the empty plate and wiped a paper napkin across his mouth.

"After this day?" She stroked the baby's head. "Jax, I just don't think I'm up to it."

"Not to worry, sweetie. I spied that box marked Books and Photos in your stuff stacked in the hall-way." Miss Delta gave a wave of her hand that made it clear that the petite powerhouse didn't mind doing a task one bit and wouldn't be deterred from it. "I'll bring it down to the kitchen, where the light is good, and we can all help you out."

"Miss Delta, you don't have to—"

In a flash of blond hair and bargain-store baubles, Miss Delta was gone.

"Why are you resisting this?" Jax picked up his plate and Shelby's and took them to the sink. "Don't you want to find Amanda's mom?"

"Yes. I do. Of course I do."

Even with his back to her and the rush of water pouring from the faucet into the sink as he rinsed the dishes, he could practically hear her squirming in her chair. When he shut the water off, he twisted his head to catch sight of her over his shoulder. "But?"

"But…" Shelby ran the back of her hand over Amanda's cheek, then along the baby's arm. She touched the tiny ballet slippers Jax had insisted on buying after Shelby's card had been turned down. "Maybe Amanda's birth mother doesn't want to be found."

He shook the dishwater off his hands, then dried them on a towel hanging from the handle of the stove. "Okay. Interesting thought. Want to tell me more?"

Not only did Shelby seem to want to tell him more, but suddenly it was as if she couldn't help herself. She got up from the table so quickly that the legs of her chair screeched over the old floor.

"What if by seeking her out, I break the trust she placed in me by leaving Amanda on my doorstep?" With Amanda in her arms, she came close to Jax, her eyes filled with concern. "What if her circumstances are such that she needs no one to know about the baby, and then I show up and ruin everything? We don't know, Jax, and if…if…"

"And if you never find Amanda's mom, you never have to give her back?" He asked it with a heart full of concern, and not an ounce of accusation.

Tears filled her eyes.

Jax went to her, putting one hand on her shoulder and one on Amanda's head. He waited until she met his gaze. "Shelby, you know that's not how this is going to go, right?"

"No, I don't know anything right now, Jax," she whispered, laying her cheek against his shoulder.

"This from the girl who stood right there telling me that when Mitch was smooth, he was lying. You heard him smooth talk his way around, knowing too much about your missing debit card, and you still wanted to believe the best of him?" He stroked her hair back from her face, kissed the top of her head and laughed softly. "How can you not believe the best of this situation?"

"With God all things are possible." She raised her head. She swiped away a tear and sniffled. "You reminded me of that when I said I wanted to change my third rule of living."

"Maybe I *should* have told you to change that third rule from 'Never trust a cowboy' to 'Quit trusting Mitch Warner.'" He pinched her chin between his thumb and forefinger, paused to soak in the warmth and beauty of her eyes, then leaned in to plant a kiss on the baby's head before he moved to the table to finish his coffee. "You're Amanda's foster parent until the state makes other arrangements. Unless you find the mother and she resigns her parental rights to the state or agrees to a private adoption."

"Is that what you want, honey?" Miss Delta appeared in the doorway with a cardboard box in her hands. "Are you honestly thinking of adopting Amanda?"

Shelby's cell phone kept her from answering. "Well, will you look at that? It's the guy who you said I should give up on." She pressed the talk button. "Hey, Mitch. What's up?"

"What does he want?" Jax took the box from Miss Delta and set it down on the table with a thud.

"He texted Courtney after we left, and he just heard back," Shelby whispered.

"He has her cell number? That would have been nice to know. Sheriff Denby might be able to—"

"Shhh." Shelby put her finger to her lips, even as she scrunched her whole face up to concentrate on the voice on the other end.

Miss Delta rushed in to take the baby and give Shelby the freedom to stick her finger in her ear and cut out the sound around her.

"Say that again, Mitch." She gasped. "That's what she said? The blackest hair she'd ever seen? Oh, Mitch, I know who that is. Thank you. Goodbye."

"You know who Amanda's mother is?" Miss Delta dropped into a kitchen chair, baby and all.

"We're looking for someone who knows me, who is old enough to have had a baby, who doesn't live in town or have anyone in town who would have known she had a baby, and has the blackest hair you've ever seen. Yeah, I know." Shelby tore open the box on the table and pulled a bright blue photo album free.

Jax moved in to look over her shoulder. Miss Delta hopped up and did the same, Amanda and all.

The pages flipped back and forth before she suddenly put her finger down just below a young girl's face. "It's Amanda."

"It *is* Amanda. She looks just like her!" Miss Delta's earrings went swinging as she shifted from looking at the photo to looking at the baby.

"If Amanda wasn't bald and chubby and a baby." Jax squinted at the photo, but he just couldn't see it.

"No. The name on the blanket. I think it wasn't meant to tell me what to call the baby. It was telling me who left her. Amanda Holden. Everyone called her Mandie." Shelby took off out of the room, calling out over the sound of her footsteps, "Amanda lived with her grandmother from summer through Christmas the year her parents split."

Jax slid the photo out from the plastic covering and checked the back for any more information. When he saw nothing, his attention drifted to another photo, this one of a fresh-faced Shelby standing by her dad and a painted sign with two hearts on it and the words The Lockhart Ranch.

Miss Delta stole a peek at it. "Look at how young Harmon looks. Shelby fell in love with that place the second she saw it."

"Loved it? I didn't think she ever lived there."

"Maybe I misspoke. She loved the *promise* of the place. After her mama died, Harmon sort of came un-moored in life, and I think she believed that ranch would give him, and her, the thing they had lost. A home."

"The promise of a home," Jax echoed. He brushed his finger over the image, feeling privileged for the glimpse into what made Shelby who she was.

"See?" Shelby came into the kitchen, holding up her backpack and the embroidered blanket they had found Amanda in. "I taught Amanda how to do embroidery just like this."

"You were wondering if she wanted you to find her or not." Jax smiled. He had noticed the similarities in stitching style that first night. He couldn't help wondering if the girl Shelby had taught had ever considered that it wouldn't be obvious to Shelby. "I think you have your answer."

Shelby took the baby they had been calling Amanda into her arms and pressed a kiss to her cheek.

Jax slid the photo of young Shelby hoping for a real home back into the album, then looked at the woman standing before him, hoping to become a real mom. "Now you have to decide what to do about it."

Chapter Thirteen

Jax left her to let it all sink in, reminding her that as an acting deputy, he had a duty to report what he had learned. He couldn't promise what that would bring. His actions might bring a swift conclusion. Or the report might get lost in the shuffle of bureaucracy and prolong things indefinitely. Identifying Amanda's birth mother would, by his estimation and personal experience with having been a ward of the state of Texas, wrest control of Amanda's situation from Shelby in favor of the state system. Even if she was allowed to keep Amanda, it would be as a foster caregiver, not as an adoptive mom.

That was worst case, of course, but still.

"Hey, it's almost supper time. We all know how happy Sheriff Denby would be to get a call asking him to come to the office so I can file a report about something Mitch Warner claimed to have been told," he had concluded. "Why don't I go pick up some things for dinner, we invite Harmon over and you think about it all?"

In other words, she needed to come to terms with the situation and decide how she would handle it—soon.

Gathering up the photo album with Mandie Holden's picture in it, she retreated to the sanctuary of her rented room and cuddled up in a large old rocking chair with baby Amanda in her arms. She hummed a lullaby, but the child did not seem one bit sleepy.

So, rocking gently, she pulled out the photo of Mandie.

"You know who this is?" She showed the old photo to the baby. "We think that's your mama. Your birth mama. Yes, we do."

Baby Amanda clapped her hands over the picture, then tried to chew on one corner.

"Well, Miss Delta does. She says you look just like Mandie." Shelby wriggled the photo free and studied the image of a young girl with long black hair, big brown eyes and olive skin. "Jax says he doesn't see it at all. I don't know. I mean, if it's not her, it would be such a coincidence, wouldn't it?"

She set the picture aside and then realized a second photo had been taken from inside the album and lay loose in the pages. She slipped it out and found herself staring into the face of her father and her younger self.

"And these people here?" She twisted her wrist around to put the photo in Amanda's sight but out of her reach. "These are the people who already love you like you are their very own flesh and blood. At least, these are *two* of the people who already love you like…" The words snagged in her throat. "You want to know who else loves you? Miss Delta, that's who. And Doc and Sheriff Andy and...Jackson Stroud."

She tucked the photo back in the album, shut it and sighed. "He may not admit it, but I can tell that man is just crazy about you, kiddo, and when he goes away, you won't ever even remember he was here."

A tear rolled down her cheek. It all seemed so very much to carry by herself. A baby. A desperate mother who put her highest trust in Shelby. A guy she had trusted, and who had broken his word countless times, would still stick around, while the one man she trusted and who had never let her down would be leaving. How did she make sense of it all?

Shelby thought of her three rules for her new life and bowed her head. Holding the baby she had come to love close to her heart, she prayed for the wisdom to know what was right and the strength to do it, to do what was best for Amanda, no matter what.

She must have drifted off to sleep after that, because the next thing she knew, the doorbell rang downstairs and it had started to get dark outside. She got up and changed the baby's diaper and put her in a sweet pink outfit, then straightened herself up and took the back stairs into the kitchen, where she found Miss Delta and Jax unloading grocery sacks.

"There she is," Harmon called with his arms spread wide. "There's my girl!"

"I'm not falling for that again, Dad." Shelby lifted the baby away from her dad and, without meaning to, placed the child right in Jax's waiting hands.

The tall man with the penetrating eyes took the child

like he'd been doing it forever, and met her gaze. "So, did you come to any conclusions while I was gone?"

"Yes," she said firmly. Clinging to the baby's tiny hand, she followed along behind Jax until he stopped, and the three of them became their own little quiet island in the big, bright kitchen. "I want somebody to tell me what to do."

"I thought you *didn't* want people doing that." Shelby's dad kicked his booted foot up to rest on his knee and tilted his chair up on two legs.

Miss Delta's mouth set in a firm line. She narrowed one eye and crossed her arms, but instead of getting after Harmon about sitting at her kitchen table properly, the woman aimed her discerning gaze at Shelby.

Jax lifted Amanda onto his shoulder, and even the baby seemed to home in on Shelby.

"I didn't want people thinking they knew what I was feeling, or volunteering me to do what they thought I should do," she corrected. "And then expecting me to do it and feel happy about it."

Harmon dropped the feet of his chair to the floor with a clunk.

Miss Delta tipped her head to the left, then to the right, sending her dangly earrings swaying.

Jax held Amanda before him, a perplexed look on his face. "Did *you* understand that, sweet thing? Because I have no idea what your foster mom just said."

Hearing Jax call her Amanda's mom touched Shelby in ways she had no idea how to defend against. That was what it had all come down to, hadn't it? She was conflicted about finding Mandie because only one of them could be Amanda's mom. "Just tell me what to do, Jax."

"I can't, Shelby Grace. Nobody can, or at least nobody should." He leaned back against the counter to touch her face lightly. "You are the one who has to live with the consequences, so you have to make this decision. What do you want?"

"What do I *want?*" To keep Amanda. To help Mandie. To know that Mitch and her father and Miss Delta were all going to be the people they truly seemed to want to be, to have the lives that God wanted them to have. She wanted Jackson Stroud to stay in Sunnyside. She wanted…a home. But none of those things were certainties. In fact, some of them were most likely never going to happen.

She shook her head. "I don't know that what I want even matters, Jax."

"It matters because until you know what you want, you aren't going to do what you need to do to make it happen." He stroked her cheek. "And all of us who love you won't be able to resist rushing in and trying to do what we think is best for you."

Shelby could feel her father's and Miss Delta's eyes on her, but she couldn't get Jax's words out of her mind. *All of us who love you.* For one fleeting moment, she thought that maybe at least some of the things she wanted could be hers. "Jax, I—"

"So you need to decide. We can take the information Mitch gave us—which amounts to a secondhand tip from an unreliable source—and turn it in to the system, and you can wait and see what happens. Or—"

"I know what I want." The instant he had said "You can wait and see," not "We," it all became clear to her. Even as she claimed to be an independent-minded woman who trusted the Lord, her whole life she had relied on other people to define her. She couldn't do both those things. She was choosing independence and trusting God. "I want to be Amanda's—the baby's—mom."

"All right! I'm gonna be a real grandpa!" Harmon sprang to his feet, took the baby from Jax's arms and began whirling her around the room.

"Oh, sweetie, that's a wonderful idea. I wish I'd had that kind of gumption when I was your age." Miss Delta rushed forward and gave Shelby a kiss on the forehead.

Shelby rolled her head just enough to look past the fringe of stiff hair-sprayed blond curls brushing her cheek and temple and find Jax, his unwavering gaze fixed on her. This was it. She was in charge. "And I want you to help me do it."

Jax called Sheriff Denby first. "I say we work backward from what we know now, and forward from what anyone in town might have known about Mandie and her grandmother years ago."

"Makes sense to me. I'll get the word out," the sheriff said in a matter-of-fact tone.

Jax covered one ear to make sure he had heard right in the clatter and chatter building around him at Miss Delta's. He raised his voice to improve the odds of being heard. "You're not coming over?"

"Sounds like you've got a handle on things there." Sheriff Denby also spoke louder than he needed to.

"I've got more than enough to do here now that we know we're looking for this Courtney girl in connection with Mitch Warner's stolen car."

"Courtney, Mitch, the car he now says was stolen showing up here on the night the baby was left, the identity thefts of customers of Miss Delta's place and the Crosspoint?" Jax shook his head. "I can't help thinking there's a connection."

"Yes, and her name is Shelby Grace Lockhart." Sheriff Denby paused to let that sink in before adding, "So you take extra care of our girl and call me if you find out anything more."

They hung up with that thought in Jax's mind. Shelby was the point where all this intersected. He had worried initially that this put her at risk of physical danger. Now, having come to know her, he knew she had put herself in danger—not of physical harm but of having her heart broken. He would do anything to protect her from enduring that again. That meant he had to find this Amanda and convince the young woman to make her wishes for Shelby to raise the baby a reality.

Jax took the lead from that point. He spoke to everyone personally, no "Someone told me" or "I heard this or that" allowed. Between that and whatever Sheriff Denby did on his end, it didn't take long before people were simply showing up at Miss Delta's house to volunteer information. This relegated Jax to the front porch, where he could make sure he didn't miss anyone but could avoid the chaos and the crowd shuffling through the rooms and hallways inside.

"Hey, Tyler." Jax stuck out his hand to the kid who worked part-time at Miss Delta's.

Tyler, who had been standing at the foot of the front steps, fixated on his phone for at least a minute, raised his head. "Hey, man!"

Jax waited for the kid to come up the steps and shake his outstretched hand.

A car pulled up and parked on the street. Headlights flicked off. Car doors slammed. People got out and called greetings.

Tyler didn't move. Jax went down the steps and forced the issue. Taking the kid's hand, he shook it, as if to say, "Be a part of the world, kid. This is how it's done."

The man he was almost two weeks ago, when he left Dallas, would never have made that concession. That man would not have cared that some kid wasn't participating in the goodness of small town life.

"Oh." Tyler caught on and actually responded to Jax's overture with a solid grip. He even made eye contact and smiled. "My mom told me to come over and see if you needed anything from me."

Jax put his hand on the young man's shoulder, feeling like he'd accomplished a small victory. "Not sure what you could do. Unless you've recalled some details from that night you thought you saw Mitch Warner at the pump?"

The kid held up his phone, as if to say that was where his attention had been focused.

Jax nodded, mulling over whether he should say more about life going on all around them and not missing it. Around them, fireflies had begun to flicker and flit, and Jax had to strain to make out faces in the dimming light. A pang of guilt hit him. Who was he to tell someone to be more engaged in life? Up until he'd come to Sunnyside, the only reason he'd paid attention to people and his surroundings was to try to figure them out, to make his case or to keep them from getting close.

He tapped the edge of his own phone. Then had a thought. "Hey, Tyler. You were texting when I drove up to the Crosspoint the night we found Amanda. Any chance you mentioned seeing Mitch to whomever you were texting with?"

"Uh." He looked down at his phone and hit the contact icon. "Yeah. I think I did."

Jax stepped in closer, a bit stunned to see the number of contacts scrolling past under the boy's skimming thumb.

"I think I said I hoped he didn't fill up and take off," Tyler said. "Because I knew how much it would embarrass Miss Shelby for her old boyfriend to be caught stealing from Miss Delta."

"Can you check back through your old texts and find out what time that happened?"

"It'll take a couple minutes, but sure." Tyler nodded.

"Come inside and join the party while you do that." Jax gave a jerk of his head and headed up the steps.

It pleased him more than he could ever have anticipated when Tyler followed his lead, came into the foyer and actually interacted with people even as he searched through his old texts.

Shelby came up behind the young man and gave him

a friendly shake. "Hi, Tyler. The light for that's better in the kitchen. And there's food."

"Cool." Tyler didn't have to be told twice.

As he disappeared into a cluster of folks laughing and talking, Shelby sidled up to Jax, who chose to stay close to the screen door. As they stood side by side, she folded her arms and said, "You know, I worried when you started asking people to come here to talk to you directly that Miss Delta would resent the intrusion."

"Are you kidding?" Jax took the whole scene in, in a long, sweeping glance. "She's like a queen holding court. And with Harmon in the kitchen? They're putting everyone at ease, making my job easier."

Shelby looked up at him. Her face, lit by moonlight on one side and the mellow glow of the old crystal chandelier above them, took on a kind but wistful expression. "Well, if nothing else comes out of this, I will always consider it a blessing that I got to see Miss Delta get at least a taste of her lifelong dream."

Jax opened his mouth to ask something that had nothing to do with the task ahead of them. Nothing to do with figuring out anyone's motivations. Nothing to do with anything but listening to Shelby, sharing a moment with Shelby. "What do you mean?"

Shelby's eyes met his, and for a moment he thought she might just shrug it off, but when she spoke softly, almost achingly, about Miss Delta's dream, he understood why.

"You know that Miss Delta said she always wanted to have a home filled with love and family here in Sunnyside."

She might as well have been talking about herself. Jax had no doubt about that. It touched his heart, but it also set off an alarm in his head. He might have made that dream come true for one night for Miss Delta, but he couldn't do the same for Shelby. His future lay down a different path.

So he did his best to redirect the conversation. "I was asking what you meant by 'if nothing else comes out of this'?"

"I mean…" She blinked. Tears washed over those beautiful blue eyes. Her lower lip quivered. She tipped her chin up, and in an instant her composure returned and she spoke with grace and acceptance. "I mean that even if we find Mandie, Jax, there is no way of knowing how it will all turn out."

He should have been relieved. He had thought the same things again and again, but hearing it from Shelby, it got to him. He took her in his arms and held her close, hoping to provide some comfort as he said, "I know. But, Shelby Grace, I have to believe it will be okay. Clearly Mandie wanted you to have Amanda. We just have to make that happen through the proper channels."

For a moment she just stood there in his arms.

Jax wondered if he had crossed a line. If he should let go, back away and make a joke or—

Shelby wound her arms around him, tentatively at first, then tightly. She buried her face in his chest. She did not cry, but sighed the way someone does when they finally surrender their burdens, if only for a little while.

Jax closed his arms around her and laid his cheek against the soft waves of her hair. He inhaled the scent of her and the night and the aroma of home cooking, and felt the loneliness of his past melt away. He might not carry that feeling for the rest of his life, but he would have this memory.

"Uh, sorry to break this up, y'all." Tyler stood beside them, his phone in one hand, a grilled cheese sandwich in the other. "But I got that text time for you, Jax."

Jax reluctantly pulled away from Shelby.

She let her hand drag across his arm as she moved back. With each step, her smile grew from weak to re-assuring.

Jax smiled, too, then checked the phone. "Okay, I wasn't expecting this."

"Everything okay?" Tyler asked.

"Yeah, that was a lot of help. Thanks, Tyler." He patted the kid on the back to send him on his way. When the young man slid the phone into his pocket and joined a group talking in the parlor, Jax shook his head and scowled. "Something's off here, Shelby. And it goes back to Mitch and his story about this mysterious Courtney. According to the time of Tyler's text, he saw that red car at nine thirty-nine. The silver SUV ran me off the road around ten thirty-five. There is almost no chance that Mandie sat in a big silver SUV at the café for at least an hour with nobody noticing."

"I admit I was distracted that night, but it doesn't seem likely, does it?" Shelby pivoted just enough to stare out the screen door at all the vehicles parked out-side, as if confirming she would have noticed the SUV in that amount of time. "Wait! *I* missed a call in the middle of the night from an unknown number. Is there some way to trace it and see if it was Mandie?"

"Let's see." He held his hand out. "Give me your phone."

Even after handing over her phone, Shelby's fingers flitted around the edge of the small device resting in Jax's palm.

"Even though it showed up unknown, the police can find out the number, right?" she asked.

Jax saw the time and date. "They can, but they won't have to."

"Why?"

He pulled his own phone out and flicked the screen on. "Because I'm the one who called you that night."

"You?"

"Yeah, I'd just found your note and…" The memory of reading her words and knowing he had to come back to her twisted in his gut. "And I called to tell you I was coming back."

"I see," she whispered.

"Maybe I should add my number to your contact list to keep that from happening again." He wasn't asking to do it; he was telling her that they needed to have each other's information because it wouldn't be long before he'd be gone again.

"Thanks." The tremor in her voice told him she understood the implications of his offer. "I'd hate to feel like every time I got a call from an unknown number, I might think it's you, telling me you're coming back."

Jax froze. He stared at her phone in his hands because he couldn't look at her. He wanted to say something, but what?

"The lady told me to speak to the deputy?" A middle-aged woman came marching down the hall, aimed directly at them. Just before she got to Jax, she stopped and gave him a puzzled look. "But you're the busboy at the café, aren't you?"

"I'm both," he admitted, a little glad for the interruption. "And, honestly, I'm neither."

She frowned.

"If you find that confusing, imagine how *I* feel." Jax laughed.

Shelby laughed, too, and hers sounded as strained and hollow as his had.

The woman shook her head and jumped in with what she had to say. "I bought Louella Holden's old house. I have contact information for her son. Would that be any help?"

"Everything new that we learn is helpful." Jax put his hand on her shoulder. "This might just be the information that brings this whole case together."

Miss Delta came waltzing by to offer a glass of tea as he slipped into a quiet room to make a quick call to Louella's son. It was a brief conversation, and filled with tension, but he did find out where Mandie was living now—and one other thing, which shook his whole system of looking for motivations in people to the core.

Chapter Fourteen

He motioned for Shelby to follow him to the back porch. They stepped into the serenity of the late spring night, and the chaos filling the old house seemed a million miles away. So did her fears and anxieties. She inhaled the smell of wonderful food, night-blooming flowers and Jax's aftershave. Years from now, when someone asked her what she remembered about the stranger who had come to town and had found the baby she hoped would then be her daughter, she would think of this moment. She knew it.

Jax leaned against the railing and held up his phone. "I spoke to Mandie's father."

Shelby closed her eyes to say a quick prayer for peace and good judgment, no matter what followed from this moment on. She opened her eyes and squared her shoulders. "Did you get her number?"

"I certainly hope not." He shook his head. "Shelby, Mandie's father hasn't spoken to her in years."

"Years?" She tried to comprehend that. "I can't tell

you how many times that summer someone would say to me that Mandie came from a broken home. I guess I had no idea how broken."

"He knew nothing about any baby, though the idea seemed far-fetched to him."

Shelby chewed her lower lip for a moment before admitting, "You know, it does to me, too. Nothing about leaving a baby in the night fits with the girl I knew."

"Her father had no phone number for her, but he could tell me that when he and his second wife split three years ago, she stayed in Westmoreland to finish her senior year of high school. He believed Mandie could still live there." Jax curved his hand around her shoulder and lowered his head, putting them eye to eye. "Because last he heard, she'd been living with her stepsister, Courtney. Oh, got a last name on her, too, finally. Collier."

Shelby's breath stopped. Just stopped, as if the wind had been knocked out of her.

"Mandie and Courtney…" She tried to make the pieces fit together. "You think Mandie was part of it all, of stealing from my bank account?"

Jax didn't say a word.

That told Shelby more than she wanted to know, so she decided to tell him a thing or two. "I don't believe that. I can't. Not for one minute, and I think we need to find her and get this all sorted out as soon as possible. How do we do that?"

"We could find a place to set up a laptop around here and do some searching online and see what we come up with. Or…" He held up a scrap of paper. "We could sneak out of here, get in my truck, drive out to this address and see what we find."

"Let's do it."

Of course, they couldn't really sneak away. As an acting deputy, Jax had to let the sheriff in on their plan, such as it was. And Shelby had to get Miss Delta to agree to take care of baby Amanda. Still, they managed to do that without telling her, or anyone else at the house, why they needed to dash off.

"You know, some people will jump to conclusions about why we left," Jax told her as he opened the door to his truck and offered his hand to help her climb in.

She hesitated, stole a look back at Miss Delta's bustling Victorian, then slid her hand into his. "Let them talk. People will do what they do. You can't stop them. You can only love them and live so that no matter what they say, you know God is pleased with your choices."

She stepped up into the cab. When she settled in, she found Jax still standing in the open door, inches away.

"What?" she asked.

He leaned in from the shoulders up, close enough now that she could see the muscles in his cheek twitch, as if he were holding back a grin. "Just a week caring for Amanda has changed you, Shelby."

"For better or worse?" she whispered.

"I honestly didn't think you could get any better," he said in a voice almost as still and quiet as hers. "But you have."

She broke away from the intensity of his searching gaze. "Everyone can always grow for the better, Jax."

"See? There you go again, better and better." He

chuckled deeply in that engaging way he had. Pushing away from the truck, he slammed the door shut.

Shelby took advantage of his absence to fan her cheeks, which she hoped hadn't gone positively scarlet over the man's nearness.

Seconds later, Jax got behind the wheel and shut his own door. His presence seemed to fill the cab of the truck, and when he started the engine and looked her way, his gaze homed in on her as keenly as his observation. "'Everyone can always grow for the better' is not the sentiment of a girl who wrote about never trusting again, who decided to give up on her dad and friends and hometown rather than believe she could find her dream right here with them."

Shelby mulled that over as they drove in tense silence through the darkness toward both Amanda and Courtney's last known address. It wasn't until they turned onto the street and Shelby noticed Sheriff Andy's official car parked a few houses away that she finally spoke up again. "I wish Sheriff Denby didn't have to be in on this. Won't it send the message she's in trouble?"

"She *is* in trouble, Shelby." Jax pulled into the center of the driveway. "If she left the baby or did any of this, or knew about it and did not turn her stepsister in, there are plenty of ways she could be very much in trouble."

Suddenly Shelby realized that Jax, and even Sheriff Andy, saw this so differently from how she did. The sheriff had parked out of sight to avoid tipping anyone off. Jax had parked in a way that would keep anyone from getting a car out of the garage and taking off.

"I get that Mandie is also a very troubled girl." He

pressed a button to lower the truck's window as Sheriff Andy came up the walk. Clearly he planned to talk with the man without the telltale sound of the truck doors closing to signal their arrival. "That doesn't change the fact that she abandoned a baby, or that there's some connection to Courtney, who at the very least is accused of stealing a car."

What she had told Jax about loving people and doing what the Lord expected weighed heavily on her heart. "If I could just talk to her..."

"The law is not devoid of mercy, Shelby, especially in Andy Denby's hands," he reminded her.

"I know."

"By seeing this through the proper way, Mandie can get what she needs—counseling, medical aid, legal advice," Sheriff Andy chimed in as he reached down and quietly opened her door. "Keep that in mind when you talk to her."

"Shelby? You want to send Shelby in first? Alone?" Jax shifted in the seat with enough pent-up energy to rock the whole truck gently.

Sheriff Andy stepped back to swing the door open. "Shelby is with us because Shelby *needs* to be with us, not just for her own interests, son."

Jax gripped the steering wheel. He didn't offer further objections, but he didn't have to—his concern about her involvement created a palpable prickle in the air around them.

"It will be okay." Shelby reached out and gave his arm a squeeze. "You're going to be right here if I need you."

The strain in his posture eased. He leaned over in the seat to put his mouth near her ear, saying with conviction, "Count on it."

"I want to," she murmured.

For just that moment in the darkened closeness of the truck's cab, Shelby wanted him to know that even though she understood it couldn't last, she believed with all her heart she could count on him.

He leaned closer still, close enough for a sweet stolen kiss.

Shelby shut her eyes in anticipation.

"Aren't you two getting a bit ahead of yourselves?" Sheriff Andy barked from the drive.

They moved apart.

"I guess I'd better…"

"Yeah. Go." Jax cleared his throat and squared his shoulders. "I'll watch for trouble from here."

Sheriff Andy made a sweeping motion, like a footman escorting Cinderella from her coach. "We don't even know if either of the girls still lives here, or if either is home, you know."

Shelby nodded. She took a deep breath.

Jax opened his door and stepped out of the truck. She didn't even hear his boot steps on the driveway. Then he was simply at her side, his hand on her back. "I know you're scared, Shelby. Not of Mandie, but of what might happen once you confront this whole tangled-up mess of a situation."

"I can do this. I know what I want, Jax." She kept her attention fixed on the door, and on the most important thing in all of this. "I want whatever is best for baby Amanda, no matter what the cost to me."

Jax folded her into an impulsive hug. "Mandie made a good choice when she decided to leave her baby in your care."

Buoyed by his confidence and closeness, Shelby went up on tiptoe, placed a kiss on the man's cheek, then turned and hurried up the drive and onto the porch. She flexed her hand, shook out the stiffness in her reluctant fingers and rang the bell.

It felt like minutes before she heard the shuffling of feet and a woman's voice call out, "This had better not be who I think it is, because I meant it when I said I'd call the cops if I ever saw—"

The door swung open. A young woman with the blackest hair Shelby had ever seen stood in the doorway. Shelby thought she whispered the woman's name, but in the intensity of the moment, she wasn't sure she even remembered her own name. From this second forward, nothing in her life could ever be as it was before baby Amanda came into her life. Even if Mandie had no connection to the child, which seemed wildly unlikely, Shelby knew she would never rest until she had found the child's mother and set things right.

In the measure of a heartbeat, the young woman's expression went from dark as thunder to bright excitement. "Miss Shelby? I can't believe it! I'm so happy to see you."

Mandie Holden threw herself at Shelby with so much force that it carried Shelby staggering backward a step or two before she found her footing and returned the joyous embrace. "Mandie! It *is* you. You do still live here, and you look…" Shelby wriggled away to take a good long study. "You look so grown-up!"

"Twenty-one last month!" The young woman beamed.

"Twenty-one? How is that possible?" Shelby counted back all those years and realized that seven years was a bigger gap when Mandie was twelve and Shelby was nineteen. Now, instead of thinking of Amanda's birth mom as a child, she viewed her more as a contemporary. That thought empowered her more than she expected.

"We need to talk, Mandie." She was not dealing with a young girl in trouble, with no life experience, who had made a hasty emotional choice, but with someone old enough to have made better choices. Someone old enough to have asked about the baby she'd left. Those would have been the first words out of Shelby's mouth. "Can we come in?"

"We?" Mandie flipped her long black hair over her shoulder and peered out into the yard.

Shelby motioned to Sheriff Andy and Jax.

The men came forward.

"A sheriff? Oh, no, what now?" Mandie put her hand to her forehead, as if suddenly hit with a pounding headache. "Is Courtney in trouble again?"

Sheriff Andy and Jax slowed the pace of their approach as they exchanged a look that Shelby could only think meant they didn't quite buy Mandie's surprise.

"So, you still have contact with your stepsister, Courtney?" Shelby took Mandie by the arm to turn her away from the scrutiny of the two lawmen. Yes, it was a protective gesture that had good ol' softhearted

Shelby written all over it. Shelby didn't care what it looked like. She cared only about Mandie and Amanda and getting all this sorted out. "Does Courtney live here with you? When did you last see her?"

"Yes. That is, she did live here until about a week ago, when she took off." She moved ahead of them into the small house.

The furniture was a bit on the shabby side, but no more so than most people her age just starting out would have. Shelby saw no sign of extravagance that might have been bought with other people's money. She also saw no sign of a baby having lived in the home. Not even a photograph.

It tugged at her heart. "Mandie, I—"

"I don't know where Courtney is, y'all." She whirled around to face them, meeting Sheriff Andy, then Jax, then Shelby squarely in the eye as she said, "But you could probably find her if you could find that guy she's been hanging around with—"

"You know *that guy's* name?" Jax stepped forward to ask.

Mandie shook her head. "She said he *gave* her a car, and the next thing I know, the cops showed up saying he reported it stolen."

"Mitch," Shelby muttered, closing her eyes to keep from having to face Jax and from feeling like a foolhardy girl for having taken Mitch back into her life time and time again. Shelby sighed. "Look, Mandie, we didn't come here about that."

"Not *just* about that," Sheriff Andy corrected.

Shelby opened her mouth, trusting somehow that

she would find the right words for what she had to ask, but no sound came.

Jax moved in behind her, taking her tense shoulders in his big, gentle hands. He literally and figuratively had her back. "Mandie, Miss Shelby brought us all the way over from Sunnyside tonight because she needs to know… Why did you leave the baby, and what can we do to help you deal with all this?"

"The baby?" A crease formed between Mandie's dark eyebrows, even as she let out a perplexed sort of laugh at Jax's phrasing. "You mean Amanda?"

"I thought *you* were Amanda." Sheriff Andy shifted his weight. The silence of the small room amplified the creak of his black uniform shoes and gun holster.

"I am. But so is the baby Shelby is adopting. That is, that's what Courtney named her. I made her a blanket with her name on it. I kind of hoped you'd keep it—the name, not the blanket—well, also the blanket, but if you wanted to call her something else…"

"Whoa, whoa, slow down here." Jax threw his hands up in a gesture so calming and sure that everyone seemed to pause and take a breath.

"*Courtney* named her?" Jax tipped his head, leaning one ear in Mandie's direction, as if to say he wasn't sure he'd heard right. "Aren't *you* the baby's mother?"

"Me?" Mandie put both hands to her chest and stepped backward so quickly, she knocked over a plant stand with a withered cactus on it. She didn't even care when the whole thing toppled to the floor with a dull thud. She just rallied and put her fists on her hips as she asked, "Did Courtney tell you that?"

"None of us have ever even met Courtney." Shelby bent down, scooped up the poor undernourished plant, set the stand upright and put the pot back where it belonged. "All we've had to go on is a blanket with the name Amanda on it and a secondhand report of someone with the blackest hair she'd ever seen at the Crosspoint Café the night we found an abandoned baby there."

"Oh, no! Abandoned?" The younger woman looked genuinely pained at that news. She put her hand over her mouth. Her face went pale. She shook her head and sank into a nearby chair. "I should have known something was wrong. She lies about everything, you know. Of course she'd lie about this."

This time when Shelby did a visual check of the sheriff's and Jax's expressions, she saw concern.

"Abandon Amanda?" Mandie looked up at Shelby, her eyes imploring. "I just don't get why she would do that."

"We can't help you figure it out until we hear the whole story." Jax moved closer.

"Start with Courtney and the baby." The sheriff got out a pad and pen to take notes.

Mandie nodded to acknowledge their request, waited for everyone to take a seat in the small room and then began to unfurl a vivid story about her younger stepsister's many struggles after Mandie's father and Courtney's mother split. For years the family and those who wanted to help had dealt with Courtney skipping school, shoplifting, staying out late. When Courtney's mother had moved to get a fresh start, she had even allowed

Mandie and Courtney to rent the family home from her in hopes it would give them some stability.

Just a couple of years out of high school, Courtney had become pregnant. At first it seemed like just the thing to get the girl on the right path. She took care of her health, stopped drinking and smoking and went to church with Mandie a few times. The baby's father had promised they'd marry as soon as he got a job and had some money saved up.

"The baby's father? Mitch?" Jax asked.

"No. A boy she went to school with. He hung around as long as his folks paid the rent and Courtney's bills, but then after they had the baby, neither of them seemed able to take care of Amanda. Or really wanted to." Mandie looked down at the floor, her shoulders slumped. "I'd have done it, but look around here. I'm not ready for that kind of responsibility. I couldn't give the baby what she needed."

"But you thought of someone who could," Jax prompted, stealing a glance at Shelby.

Shelby pressed her lips together, fighting the urge to burst into tears at the whole story.

"I remembered how good you were with kids, Miss Shelby. How much your daddy loved you, how much everyone in town loved you. And I told Courtney about you." Mandie gave Shelby a big smile. "Courtney didn't meet this Mitch until a few weeks ago, when she started going over to Sunnyside every few days—which she told me was to meet with you about adopting Amanda."

Jax leaned forward in his chair. "Let me guess. She

also told you that Shelby was giving her money to help out with her expenses."

"Yes." She nodded, paused, then fiddled with her hair and added, "Don't tell me *that* wasn't true, either."

"She got my bank information and stole about a thousand dollars before I even knew it, Mandie," Shelby said.

"Oh, Miss Shelby!" Mandie shot up from her chair and came over to where Shelby was sitting on the couch. She knelt on the floor and folded her arms over Shelby's knees. "I must have asked her a million times if I could talk to you on her behalf or join your meetings, and she told me she wanted to do it herself, to stand on her own. It seemed like such a positive step, taking responsibility, that I… Can you ever forgive me?"

Shelby reached out and took the younger woman's hand in hers. "Forgive *you?* You did nothing wrong."

Mandie's inky black hair shimmied from side to side as she shook her head vehemently. "I feel so guilty that I couldn't get Courtney to straighten up, the way you did for me."

"I didn't do anything but spend time with you, Mandie."

"I know. You spent time on me when nobody else seemed to have any to spare for me. Now I work full-time. I'm taking some college courses. And I teach Sunday school—preschool, but it's a start."

"It's a wonderful start, Mandie!" Shelby stood and gave the young woman a hug.

"All thanks to you, Miss Shelby." Mandie hugged

her right back, and it seemed clear the meeting was winding down.

"Do you have a way to contact your stepsister?" Sheriff Andy asked, pen poised over paper. "Any idea when you might see her again?"

"Well, since this guy reported her stealing his car, and she knows people are onto her for hacking their debit and credit card accounts, it's a pretty safe bet she'll show up here before too long."

Sheriff Andy asked for a photograph of Courtney, and when Mandie found one, Shelby captured the image on her phone. Then Sheriff Andy wrapped up his part in it all and left to go coordinate what he had learned with the Westmoreland Police Department.

"Night, Miss Mandie." Sheriff Andy tipped his head to the young woman seated at Shelby's side. "Thank you for your cooperation."

He placed his hat on his head, gave Jax a look that Shelby couldn't quite decipher and let himself out.

Jax, sitting on the edge of the chair across from the couch, looking ready to spring into action at any moment, turned toward them. For the first time since he'd rushed to the aid of what he had thought were kittens in a basket on the Crosspoint's deck, he seemed uncertain about what to do next.

He slapped his hands against his denim-clad legs. He started to speak, then refrained. He appeared genuinely pleased when his phone chimed out his no-nonsense ringtone, and he tugged it from his pocket. "I should probably see who this is."

As the picture of the building in Miami spread across

the small screen, he frowned. His forehead creased and his eyes went almost squinty, as if he thought he could intimidate the object into silence.

"It's okay. We're pretty much done here. Answer it if you need to." *Need* to. Not *want* to. Shelby had chosen her words purposefully. If Jax wanted to get back to his real life, the life he was on the path to creating when he took the detour into Sunnyside almost two weeks ago, Shelby did not want to know. But doing what a person needed to do—that she understood, and she would do nothing to interfere.

His hesitation did that job for him as the call went to voice mail, indicated by a buzz and a different kind of chime.

Jax let the phone rest on the arm of the chair for a moment. He sat back in the seat, kicked his right boot up to rest on his left knee, then adjusted his position and did the opposite. Finally, his large hand hovering just above the cluster of icons on the screen, he picked up the phone.

"Ladies, if you'll excuse me?" He stood. "I've got something to take care of before we get back on the road, Shelby."

Shelby watched until he completely disappeared out the front door before she turned to Mandie again. So many things she longed to say, so many messages she wanted to give to both this young woman and to baby Amanda's birth mother. She just didn't know where to start. "I want you to know that I have loved every second of having baby Amanda in my life, and I don't know what I will do if—"

"Oh, Miss Shelby, don't even imagine that Amanda will be taken from you. The baby's father gave up his rights, and his parents were happy to have Amanda go to you."

"So Courtney has everyone believing she went through the proper channels?" The whole story saddened Shelby, but this news gave her a ray of hope. If Courtney had made her intentions to choose Shelby to raise Amanda clear, and the father and paternal grandparents had agreed to that, then in all likelihood the adoption would go through smoothly.

"They may want to see Amanda from time to time, but they're not interested in raising a baby. They told Courtney that firsthand when she would take off for days and leave Amanda with them."

"I can do that." For the first time in days, when she said she could do something, she felt sure she actually could, not just hopeful that she'd try her best.

"I'll do whatever I can with Courtney, or with the legal people, to make sure they know the baby belongs with you."

"Thank you, Mandie. That means a lot." She took the young woman's hand and gave it a squeeze. "And it would also mean a lot if you'd just call me Shelby. I don't even remember how that Miss Shelby stuff got started, but I never have liked it. It makes me sound a million years old, especially when half the town, some of them only three or four years younger than me, calls me that. Nobody asked me if I wanted to be called that. They just thought I'd like it."

"Oh, Miss Shelby, I don't know if I could."

"You *have* to," Shelby insisted, speaking up for her-self at long last. "We're friends now, and it's what I want."

"Okay then...Shelby. Everything will work out. You'll see. That sheriff will see to it that Courtney doesn't pull anything funny, and that Jax guy?" Man-die's dark eyes grew big. She let out a long low whistle and shook her head. "I don't think he'd let anybody do anything to hurt you, *ever*."

Not on purpose, she thought, but because of Jax, Shelby knew she would be hurt. And yet she knew now that she could handle it.

"With him on your side, you and Amanda have noth-ing to worry about."

Shelby almost blurted out that the Jax guy wasn't in this for the long haul. That, in fact, the call he had just gotten was most likely a summons for him to hit the road. One he had no reason not to answer, now that there wasn't anything more for him to do about find-ing out who left Amanda.

Instead, she gave Mandie a hug, reminded her to do as Sheriff Andy asked to cooperate with his inves-tigation and thanked her. Then she headed out to join Jax, knowing that she had another goodbye in her near future.

Chapter Fifteen

Though Shelby had smiled all the way through the five-minute-long hug fest filled with thank-yous, encouragements and promises to keep in touch, as soon as the truck hit the highway headed back to Sunnyside, she began to cry softly. The tears flowed the whole way back, and Jax didn't say or do anything to try to stop them. Shelby deserved to have this time to just let go, to not have to fear the repercussions of showing her emotions.

He couldn't change the situation with Courtney or Mitch or Amanda. He could, however, protect her from the assumptions and expectations of practically everyone in Sunnyside.

He stole a glance her way.

She twisted around in the seat, keeping her face to the side window, but the shiver in her shoulders and a slight sniffle gave away that she hadn't worked through things yet. He'd seen this time and again in people of strong character, strong determination and even strong faith. They kept moving forward, allowing nothing to deter them from their goal, then often lost control when it all came to a conclusion—even a happy conclusion.

The truck's headlights slashed across a sign advertising Buffalo Betty's Chuck Wagon Ranch House.

"Hey, maybe when all this is settled, you and Mandie can take Amanda back to the restaurant and—"

"I don't think so," she said quietly.

"I know it's a lot to process. But you're on the downhill side now." He believed that, and it gave his words renewed energy as he assured her, "Once Sheriff Andy files official charges of child abandonment against Courtney, things should be on track for you to start the process of becoming Amanda's mom, right?"

"I know. I'm relieved about all that." The heaviness of her sigh belied that claim. "Mandie said over and over that Courtney has no interest in keeping the baby, that the time she had Amanda made her see she wasn't ready for parenthood."

"I hope that's true, but…" Jax wished he could tell her there wouldn't be bumps along the way, but he had dealt with people like Courtney over and over in his experiences in the foster care system and as a cop. There were so many unknowns at play, so many possible outcomes. He believed with all his heart that Shelby would fight for what was best for Amanda and that it would work out, but he couldn't pretend she wasn't in for a struggle. "When this all catches up with her, you realize that Courtney could use severing Amanda's parental rights as a bargaining chip."

"I don't care. I still want to work things out for

Amanda." She sat up straight in the seat and shook her hair back like a woman filled with new resolve as she added, "And for Courtney."

"For Courtney?"

"Yes. For Courtney." She shifted in the seat just enough to angle her upper body toward him. Her whole face took on that fierceness he had seen in her that first night, when she thought she was standing up to the kind of man who would leave a baby on a doorstep. "This is Amanda's birth mother, Mandie's stepsister. I know she's made a lot of mistakes, but it sounds like she's had a lot of people let her down in life, Jax."

It took everything in him not to bust out in a big old grin as she spoke.

"I just hope she gets a chance at redemption, at making up for those mistakes," she went on. As she looked out the side window again, her voice grew softer. "That's all. I want everyone in this to know God's love and mercy and to have a better life."

"Of course you do."

Shelby whirled her head about so fast, Jax half expected to hear the sound of a whip cracking. Her eyes all but shot fire. He'd seen *that* look before, and it made his heart sing.

"Are you making fun of me, Jackson Stroud?"

"That's the furthest thing from my mind," he said with quiet conviction. He had always looked for people's worst motivations as part of his work, and as an excuse not to get close to them, he now understood. Shelby didn't look for shortcomings in anyone, and even when presented with them, she considered how to help eir issues. Jax was better for

thinking how much I admire
much I've learned from you
nown each other."

to say something sassy—he
posture and the flush in her
t passed, and as his confes-
e went a bit gushy, pulling her
er head to one side. "Really?"

esitating to confirm his state-
efore he said what he knew
id when he spoke, he kept his
stealing a glimpse to see how
d because of that, I know it's
o leave now."

sk anything more about his
ad again, and they drove on
ng into Sunnyside.

ay to Miss Delta's house," she
street he had just passed.

phone call I made. I asked
da and meet us at the café."
ound to the back lot that the
with Miss Delta's Shoppers'
Stop Inn, as if he'd done that
for years. "I wanted to give
e yourself and not have to do

id whispered, "Thank you for

"And I wanted to tell her goodbye."

Jax pulled his truck into a spot that allowed him to see the street and know when Harmon arrived with the baby. He knew it would not be long, and he wanted to make the most of this last little time he had alone with Shelby.

She sniffled and tugged a tissue out of her purse. "I grabbed a wad of these from Miss Delta's house because I thought I'd need them for Mandie."

Always thinking of others first, Jax thought. He decided not to say it, in case it might make her feel defensive. In his book, this woman needed no defense of her emotions or actions. "Shelby Grace, in case I haven't made it clear already, meeting you, spending time with you, well, you...*you* have changed me for the better."

"Oh, Jax, that's..." She gave him the shiest of smiles, then opened her door and gave a not quite convincing laugh. "That's a pretty big responsibility to lay on my shoulders."

He opened his door and climbed out of the truck. Over the solid clunk of both doors falling shut, he called out to her, "I thought it was a compliment."

"Oh, it is." She rummaged in her purse for a minute, then retrieved her cluttered key ring. It jangled in her hand as she started toward the darkened café. "I am so humbled that you think that, but you know what I think?"

He didn't follow her. "What?"

She turned and put her hands on her hips. "That maybe I was just an instrument of the Lord in whatever has affected you this week."

"That's fair." He nodded.

She gave a little bow, like a diva accepting an ovation, then turned and headed toward the café, her steps crunching in the gravel of the small lot.

Jax watched her retreating. There, with only the bright moon to light their way, Jax could not see any telltale signs as to her mood or mind-set. But he didn't have to. In just this short time, he had come to understand Shelby Grace Lockhart in ways he had never understood another person alive.

He planted his own feet in the gravel and, even as they settled in slowly, unevenly, called out after her, "But I hope you recognize that by being you, by having the kind of heart that's open to so much love, you gave the Lord a lot to work with."

Her steps slowed, then stopped. She cast a look at him over her shoulder.

He went to her, brushed her hair back with one hand and said, "I will never forget you, Miss Shelby Grace Lockhart."

"Oh, Jax. That's the sweetest thing anyone has ever said to me." She looked up at him, a smile on her lips but the threat of tears in her eyes. She laid her palm on his cheek, then let her hand fall to the side of his neck, his shoulder. Then she lifted it away and smacked him hard once on the upper arm. "I can't believe you waited until you had to go to say it."

"Hey, I thought I was being nice!" He rubbed his arm, even though he had barely felt the blow.

"Being nice just before you say goodbye is…is… It's just crummy, that's what it is. Now every time I think of this time and your part in it, this is what I'll think of. Not all the good, just the goodbye! It's a rotten thing to do to a girl, Jax, to leave her with that kind of—"

Before she could get another breath to press on with her rant, Jax stepped in, wound his arms around her and kissed her. Not the quick, tender kisses they had shared along the way, but a real kiss. A goodbye kiss.

The seconds went by, counted out by their beating hearts, and the kiss ended.

Shelby tried to push away from him, but he held her just a moment longer. "Whenever I think about my time in Sunnyside, that's what *I'll* remember."

Stay. If she just said that one word, Jax might actually...might actually have to tell her no. He had a contract. People counting on him. Shelby had a lot to work out here, and trying to fit in a relationship on top of it all wasn't fair to her.

Shelby had had enough of other people using her good nature to get what they wanted. Jax couldn't be another one. He had to leave Sunnyside, for Shelby's own good.

The glow of headlights turning into the lot from the road made Jax let go and move away.

Shelby bowed her head and did the same.

Less than a minute later they were in the café, Miss Delta, Harmon, baby Amanda, Shelby and Jax.

"Hey, beautiful," Jax whispered as he took the baby in his arms one last time. "I know you won't remember me, but I hope you know that I'll be praying for you every day, just like I did the night we found you.

Praying that you will find your way. Praying that you will be happy."

Any further words caught in Jax's throat. He clenched his teeth tight and settled for just giving the child a kiss on the head. When he saw Sheriff Denby slip in through the unlocked back door, he handed the baby back to Shelby, lingered a moment with the two of them, then headed over to resign.

"Not going to stay and see this to the finish, then?" Denby asked before he would take the silver badge glinting in the overhead lights of the café.

"I made a promise to be in Miami. This is one cowboy who always keeps his promises," he said.

"I guess I was wrong about you." Miss Delta shook her head.

"How so?" Jax asked as he fit his Stetson on, preparing to get back on the road, to get on with the life he had planned before this detour.

"I thought you were where you needed to be. Seems like it was only where you ended up on your way to where you needed to be." She gave him a sad smile, then stretched up to give him a kiss on the cheek. "I hope you find what you're looking for at your next stop."

Jax hoped so, too, though he sincerely doubted he would.

"So, you're really going to go. I guess you got your answer, then?" Denby flipped the badge over in his open palm.

"Why Shelby Grace? Yes, because everybody trusts her and she deserves that trust." The answer came quickly to Jax's lips.

"I wasn't asking that question literally, son." The older man shoved the badge into his shirt pocket, then gestured toward Shelby at the counter, talking to her father. "I was asking if it wasn't worth finding out why, out of all the people in the whole wide world, someone, anyone, would leave a baby with Shelby Grace Lockhart."

Shelby moved the baby to her other shoulder, her cheek brushing the baby's cheek, her eyes glittering with delight and maybe the beginning of tears.

Jax nodded. He didn't know if he smiled or if his eyes reflected the emotions of the moment. He took a deep breath and answered Denby's question simply. "I think I know why."

"And you're still gonna leave, anyways?" The older man shook his head.

The question hit Jax like a sucker punch to the gut. Rather than let anyone, even someone who had been as close to a father figure as Jax had ever had, see how much it cost him to leave Shelby, he made a joke. "You just want me to stay so you can groom me to take over your job so you can retire."

"That your fancy big-city police-procedure detective training talking, son, or that gut feeling about why people do what they do that you claim to have?"

"Little bit of both." Jax adjusted his hat and shifted his boots in line with the shortest way to the door.

"Hmm." The sheriff studied him with his lips pursed; then he lifted his shoulders and gave a shrug that somehow conveyed more disappointment than disinterest.

"You'd think between the two of them, you'd have done a better job figuring out what was going on."

Jax met the sheriff's eyes. He couldn't tell if the man was joking or not.

"What I want, son, what *any* man who serves and cares about people wants, is what's best for *them,* not himself." He put his hand on Jax's back. "Count it as a blessing if they work out to be the same thing."

Jax nodded. "I will."

"Got no reason to believe that, son." His expression said he wished he could believe it. "You haven't so far."

Jax wanted to argue with the man, but the tough-as-leather sheriff gave a snort, shook his head, turned and walked away, leaving Jax standing there, all alone among people he had known only a few days, but whom he cared about more than he could express.

So he left it at that, left anything else he felt or hoped unsaid. He raised his hand and told them that if he left right away, he could be in Miami by tomorrow afternoon.

Shelby moved toward him, but he held up his hand to hold her off. They had said their goodbyes. He didn't think he could go through another one and still get in that truck and leave.

And he had to leave. For Shelby's sake.

Chapter Sixteen

By Friday of his first full week on the new job, Jax had already begun to count out his days in terms of "How long until lunch?" "How long until my next break?" "How long until quitting time?" Except with this new job, there was no quitting time. More than once, that had made him think of Sheriff Denby's halfhearted complaints about working in a small town. Jax knew the man had loved his years of service, and was loved and respected in return for all he gave.

Here there was no respect to speak of, and certainly no love. No respect for boundaries. No consideration of him as a person, deserving of personal time or basic personal pleasantries, like learning his name.

Before his time in Sunnyside—before Shelby Grace Lockhart—that would have been just fine with him. Now when most people who bothered to speak to him, usually to demand something, called him Jack, or worse, Jackie, he cringed. To be fair, he hadn't learned the names of many of the people in the gated community, either. He tended to think of them by descriptions of their houses—the yellow villa on Bradford Street. Or by their cars—Mr. Leave a Space between That Truck and My Jag. He had never once tried to figure any of them out. Why they did what they did just did not interest him.

In fact, he had spent more time in these past few days trying to figure out why he had done what he had than ever before in his whole life. He thought it was for Shelby, but now with the gift of time and distance, he had to wonder. Had he really put her first—or used that as an excuse?

It must have been the right thing to do, he argued. If it hadn't been, wouldn't Shelby have called and asked him to come back?

"Why?" he heard himself whisper in the silence of his truck cab, where he'd gone to sit during his afternoon break to check his phone messages.

The answer to his question did not come, so he settled for who, what, where and when as told in texts and missed calls from Denby, Miss Delta, even Tyler.

"Courtney Collier turned herself in yesterday. She said she had a change of heart and wanted to do the right thing. I suspect that Mandie got Shelby Courtney's phone number, and our girl's been doing what she does so well. She may just love that lost lamb right back into the fold yet. If anyone can do it…" Denby had paused, as if he wanted to make sure Jax took a minute to let that sink in. Then the older man had cleared his throat and added, "Just thought you'd like to know."

Next came a call from an attorney who would be

working on Shelby's petition to adopt Amanda, with a request to speak to him to get a statement about the night they found the baby. It made him smile to know things had begun to get resolved, and Shelby was making progress toward becoming Amanda's mom.

Tyler sent a quick text: Can I ask Mandie Holden out even if I have to testify against her stepsister, or is that against some law?

"Yeah, against the law of probability that she'll say yes." Jax chuckled, then felt badly that the kid might get shot down. He tapped in the only answer that he could think of, then let his thumb linger a moment over the send icon before he touched it and sent the message: Okay to ask but maybe you should talk to Miss Shelby first. She'll have your answers.

Miss Delta had called to say that it seemed wrong to charge him for that last night because he didn't actually use his room at the Truck Stop Inn. She wanted to send him a refund if he'd give her his new address. "Oh, and by the way, that Mitch Warner wanted to move into your room at the inn. Harmon was all set to run him off, but Shelby beat him to it. Said he was one cowboy she had learned could not be trusted."

"That's my girl," he whispered with a small laugh. "That's my Shelby Grace. *My* Shelby Grace," he repeated, this time not finding even the hint of amusement in the term.

He took a deep breath and leaned his head back, his eyes shut. When he had first heard of this job and decided it was the thing he needed to get away from Dallas, where people had begun to actually care about him, he hadn't even heard of Shelby Grace Lockhart. Now it seemed everything, even his misery in this place, this job, came back to her.

If only he could hear her voice again. If she would just call...

"Hey! Jack! What're you doing out here?" A sharp rapping on the window inches from his face gave Jax a start. He turned to find the president of the neighborhood association red-faced and beady-eyed, with his nose almost pressed against the window as he blustered, "Have you forgotten why you came here?"

Jax pressed a button, and the window rolled down with a steady whir. "What did you ask me? *Why?*"

That was the big question that had dominated Jax's life. Why did he take this job? Why did he take the turnoff to Sunnyside that night? Why was he here?

Why Shelby Grace Lockhart? Sheriff Denby's question. The question that had compelled him to stay in Sunnyside when it was not a part of his plans came ringing back in his mind.

That question was easy to answer. People came to Shelby because she had a servant's heart. She didn't just say it, but she believed that with God all things were possible. And despite what she said about trusting cowboys, she trusted God more than her fears.

If Jax's heart was changed by knowing her, why was he on the same path he'd started down before they'd ever met?

"I came here because I thought living in a place where I got a big check to always stay a stranger was the way to keep from ever losing anyone again. The way

I lost my mom or all the foster families I lived with."
Jax swung the truck door open, more to encourage the
other man to back off physically than because he intended to get out. "I thought this place sounded like a
dream come true."

"If you want to go on drawing those big checks,
you'd do well to do your job." The man pulled his shoulders up with enough force to make his thinning hair
waft out of place, revealing his receding hairline. "Not
sit in your vehicle, wasting time on the phone."

Jax looked at the device in his hand and realized
there was one more call in the voice-mail queue. "My
Shelby Grace."

"What? Did you hear me?" the man barked.

But Jax couldn't hear anyone or anything but the
voice on the other end of the line saying, "What are
you doing? You know better than…Jax? Jax, I'm sorry.
Amanda must have dialed your number. I, uh, I don't
know if I ever told you thank you, but in case I didn't…
thanks for helping me figure out what I want in life and
telling me not to be afraid to go for it. I hope you're
doing the same."

Shelby had stood up to Mitch; she had worked to help
Courtney no matter what others might have thought of
that. She didn't need him to leave to do those things.
They were in her all along. It wasn't her needs that had
caused him to leave Sunnyside, but his. What had mo-
tivated him? Fear? Grief?

He had to ask himself, what was in him? Was he a
man of faith and service? Was he a family man or…

"This time is coming out of that big paycheck you

say you came here to get." The man tapped his gleaming gold watch, then turned to storm off.

"Yeah, well, what if I don't care about those checks anymore?" Jax climbed out of the truck and took a good long look at his surroundings. They had every luxury, every convenience, and not one single thing that mattered to him. "What if my dreams have changed?"

The man blustered a moment, then stabbed his finger in Jax's direction. "You just don't forget your place, you hear me?"

"Yes, actually, I do. I hear you loud and clear, and I think that's very sound advice."

Shelby finished filling the last of the ketchup bottles in the café and twisted the cap on tight. With the expenses of the adoption process looming ahead of her, she was happy to pitch in whenever Harmon needed a hand, especially at night, when Miss Delta was all too happy to watch over the baby. They had almost finished closing up when a flash of headlights drew her attention. She checked the clock. "It's almost eleven. Should I lock the door?"

"Do it," Harmon called back. "Tyler's still got some customers. If somebody's hungry, they can grab a snack over there. I'm bushed."

"Not too bushed to go over and visit the baby, like you do every night, I bet," she joked as she headed to the door to turn the lock.

"I love my granddaughter," he called back as he hung up his apron and reached for his beat-up old straw cowboy hat hanging on the wall.

"And it doesn't hurt that when you visit her, you get to spend time with Miss Delta, does it?" After all these years, for her father and Miss Delta to have realized their happiness might just be right here in Sunnyside with each other warmed Shelby's heart. It also made her wonder about her own future.

She stole a peek through the blinds on the café door, looking past the lot with a cluster of vehicles still in it to the road that led to the highway and beyond. "After all the papers are signed, Amanda and I can live anywhere, can't we?"

"You thinking of running off somewhere, sweetheart?" Harmon snapped off the lights, and the café went dark except for a faint glow from the light kept constantly burning in the kitchen.

For one fleeting moment, that thought took Shelby back to the night she had thought her only chance to make a life for herself lay in running away. She closed the blinds and shook her head. "No. I belong here. Amanda belongs here. That doesn't mean there won't ever be times that I won't look in the direction of, say, Florida and wonder—"

A scuffing noise outside the door cut her off. She acted quickly and swung the door open.

"Sorry, we're..." A dull *thunk* and a gray cowboy hat tumbling backward on the café's front deck made her gasp. She raised her eyes, and her heart stopped. "Closed."

"I can see you're closed." Jackson Stroud didn't even bother to scoop up his cowboy hat. "That's why I came here. I was hoping to catch you alone before the whole town heard I had come back and started deciding how you should feel about it and what you should—"

Shelby threw her arms around his neck and kissed him.

"Do," he said, finishing his thought when he got the chance to take a breath.

"Nobody tells me what to feel or how to act anymore, cowboy," she said, unable to keep from smiling as she looked into Jax's face.

"Good. Because I know some people might say we haven't known each other long enough for me to say this, but Shelby Grace Lockhart, I love you and I came all the way from Florida to tell you so."

"Florida," she said in a wistful, faraway voice. "I was just thinking Amanda and I might want to go there someday."

"Yeah? I hear it's a great place to take kids on a vacation."

"Or to live."

"I guess so, if that's where you belong." He wrapped his arms around her and lifted her feet off the ground. "Me? I'm kind of thinking of settling down somewhere else. Got any thoughts on a place called Sunnyside, Texas?"

"Now, what would ever motivate a man like you to do that?" She touched his cheek.

He put his nose to hers. "Did you not hear me say that I love you, woman?"

"Yeah." She smiled a smile that seemed to shine from her eyes all the way down to her toes. "I thought I did hear that."

"Funny, I didn't hear the same from you."

"Maybe if you said it aga—"

"I love you, Shelby Grace Lockhart." He set her down and kissed her. Then he kissed her again. Then he laughed and said, "I love Amanda. I love this nosy little town and the people who are, even as we speak, peering out the café and emporium windows and taking videos with their cell phones...." He glared at Tyler, standing only a few feet away. "And I have come all this way to tell you this is where I need to be, this is where I want to be and you are who I want to be here with."

"A simple 'I love you' would have been enough." She sighed. "Because I love you right back, Jackson. I love this town, too, and I want to raise Amanda here... with you."

"Shelby Grace, are you proposing to me?"

"Oh, I... That's not... I just meant..." She stepped back. "Jax, I'd never..."

"Well, I would." He got down on his knee, started to reach into his pocket, then turned back to Tyler, who was still standing nearby. "This I don't mind if you record on your cell phone."

"Yes, sir," the kid said, holding the object out.

Jax fished a small box out of his pocket and opened it as he said, "I know we haven't known each other long, but I have never felt so at home as I feel when I'm with you. Will you marry me?"

Shelby's eyes filled with tears, and her heart filled with joy. The word turned to dust in the tightness of her throat, but that did not stop her from nodding her yes.

In a heartbeat Jax swept her up in an embrace. Jax kissed her, and the people around them cheered.

"Yes," she said, louder this time. "I can't wait to start a life with you, Jax."

"You may have to write some new rules for living, you know," he teased as he slid the ring on her finger.

"Let's talk about that later." She looked at her ring, glittering in the moonlight, and laughed. "Right now, let's kiss again!"

Another cheer went up from the onlookers.

They did kiss again, then hurried off to tell Miss Delta, Sheriff Andy and Doc Lovey and, of course, to hug Amanda.

Epilogue

Six Months Later

"Who do you think should walk her down the aisle?"

"If you want my vote, I say her daddy. It's what all the cool girls are doing today." Harmon adjusted his bow tie and held his arm out properly crooked for his daughter to slip her hand through.

"Her daddy," Shelby murmured, her heart so filled with love and joy she wondered if people would see it beating through the intricate white lace of her gown. "I like that."

"Imagine how *he* feels." Harmon chuckled.

Shelby didn't have to imagine. One look at Jax's face as he stood waiting at the altar with Amanda in his arms, and she knew. The man loved her. And he loved the little girl who had toddled down the aisle, clinging to his strong, sure hand moments earlier. The little girl they had found one night when they both felt lost and alone, who would officially become their daughter right after Shelby and Jax returned from their honeymoon.

They took their vows before the Lord and everyone they loved, then headed to the Crosspoint Café for their reception. When it came time to leave and for Shelby to throw the bridal bouquet, she lifted it high, gave a wink to Mandie, her maid of honor, then picked her target out in the crowd.

"Oh!" Suddenly she froze with the bouquet over her head.

"What?" Jax asked.

She brought the bundle of roses and jasmine down and slipped a folded piece of paper out from inside the satin binding.

"There." She handed the single page to him, cocked her arm, aimed and let the bouquet fly.

Miss Delta didn't even bother pretending she thought Shelby ever planned to toss the flowers to anyone else. She caught them single-handedly, then hoisted them up like Lady Liberty with her torch. "You know what this means, Harmon Lockhart. I'm the next one to get married, and if it ain't you, then I may have to snag the next cowboy cop who happens by in the night for my own self!"

The wedding party cheered, and the party went on. Jax and Shelby slipped away, and as they got into the truck with the just-hitched sign on the tailgate, Jax unfolded the paper and read it aloud.

"To whom it may concern, and the only one it does concern, my loving husband, Jax.

I'm not going anywhere. No matter what. Because I love you and I know now there is only one rule I need to make a life with you."

"With God all things are possible," he said without having to even read it.

"With God all things are possible," she echoed.

And with one more kiss, they left the café behind them, though only for a five-day honeymoon, and started their new life as husband and wife.

* * * * *

If you enjoyed this story by Annie Jones,
be sure to check out the rest of the
Love Inspired books out this month!

Dear Reader,

It will be no surprise to you after reading *Bundle of Joy* that I have a soft spot for babies. And cowboys. As a mom who is now seeing friends and family become grandparents, I get my baby fix often enough, and once a year a visit home to Oklahoma reminds me why I love those cowboys.

You might also gather that I love small towns with charming characters and cafés. I have lived mostly in small towns the past fifteen years and can say there has never been a shortage of any of those things. I especially adore my own small town's efforts to keep the downtown area updated without losing its sense of history. So it was an easy choice to find the romance in all that and to share those things with readers.

Along the way I found myself putting in some glimpses into my former life as a caregiver for children in need, and to honor the many people I know who have been part of the adoption process. Helping children is a difficult and often thankless job, and I want to shower those who do it with appreciation.

I hope you enjoyed *Bundle of Joy* and that your life is blessed with friends, family, happy surprises and joy by the bundle!

Annie Jones

Questions for Discussion

1. Both Jax and Shelby think that moving away is the only chance they have to live the way they want. Have you ever felt this way?

2. Shelby feels that other people are keeping her from realizing her dreams, and she must change that. What is the negative side to this kind of thinking? The positive?

3. Because Jax is suspicious of people's motivations, he wants to live a life helping people without letting them get to know him. What do you think would be the result of living like this?

4. A baby on a doorstep is an old story line. Have you ever heard of someone actually finding a baby? What emotional impact did the story have on you and others?

5. Miss Delta chose a life serving others in her small town, where she was happy, over going out to seek someone to love. Would you have made the same choice?

6. Do you think the story portrayed a small community accurately?

7. Shelby worked as a waitress while saving for her dream. Have you ever had a job you considered just

temporary until you saved up enough to go on to something better? What was it?

8. What do you think was the greatest takeaway or lesson of the story?

9. Shelby was a longtime Sunday school teacher who had a big impact on her students. Have you ever taught Sunday school or something similar? Did you have a special student you will always remember?

10. The sheriff doesn't want to retire until he can find someone who will serve the town properly. Have you ever had a job you knew you should leave but couldn't because of the people who counted on you?

11. Did you have a teacher who had a long-lasting impact on you? Who was it? How did they affect you?

12. What about the romance felt the most realistic to you? What was most romantic part of the story, in your opinion?

13. Did you think Jax would honor his contract and leave, or did you think he'd break it and stay without going to his new job? Which would you have done?

14. Did you enjoy the book? Who was your favorite character?

REQUEST YOUR FREE BOOKS!

2 FREE INSPIRATIONAL NOVELS
PLUS 2
FREE
MYSTERY GIFTS

Love Inspired™

YES! Please send me 2 FREE Love Inspired® novels and my 2 FREE mystery gifts (gifts are worth about $10). After receiving them, if I don't wish to receive any more books, I can return the shipping statement marked "cancel." If I don't cancel, I will receive 6 brand-new novels every month and be billed just $4.49 per book in the U.S. or $4.99 per book in Canada. That's a saving of at least 22% off the cover price. It's quite a bargain! Shipping and handling is just 50¢ per book in the U.S. and 75¢ per book in Canada.* I understand that accepting the 2 free books and gifts places me under no obligation to buy anything. I can always return a shipment and cancel at any time. Even if I never buy another book, the two free books and gifts are mine to keep forever.   105/305 IDN FVV7

Name _____ (PLEASE PRINT)

Address _____ Apt. #

City _____ State/Prov. _____ Zip/Postal Code

Signature (if under 18, a parent or guardian must sign)

Mail to the Harlequin® Reader Service:
IN U.S.A.: P.O. Box 1867, Buffalo, NY 14240-1867
IN CANADA: P.O. Box 609, Fort Erie, Ontario L2A 5X3

Are you a subscriber to Love Inspired books
and want to receive the larger-print edition?
Call 1-800-873-8635 or visit www.ReaderService.com.

* Terms and prices subject to change without notice. Prices do not include applicable taxes. Sales tax applicable in N.Y. Canadian residents will be charged applicable taxes. Offer not valid in Quebec. This offer is limited to one order per household. Not valid for current subscribers to Love Inspired books. All orders subject to credit approval. Credit or debit balances in a customer's account(s) may be offset by any other outstanding balance owed by or to the customer. Please allow 4 to 6 weeks for delivery. Offer available while quantities last.

Your Privacy—The Harlequin® Reader Service is committed to protecting your privacy. Our Privacy Policy is available online at www.ReaderService.com or upon request from the Harlequin Reader Service.

We make a portion of our mailing list available to reputable third parties that offer products we believe may interest you. If you prefer that we not exchange your name with third parties, or if you wish to clarify or modify your communication preferences, please visit us at www.ReaderService.com/consumerschoice or write to us at Harlequin Reader Service Preference Service, P.O. Box 9062, Buffalo, NY 14269. Include your complete name and address.

LI13

SPECIAL EXCERPT FROM

Love Inspired **HISTORICAL**

When a tragedy brings a group of orphans to a small
Nebraska town, shy schoolteacher Holly Sanders is
determined to find the children homes...and soften dour
sheriff Mason Wright's heart, along the way!
Read on for a sneak preview of

FAMILY LESSONS by Allie Pleiter,
the first in the ORPHAN TRAIN series.

"You saved us," Holly said, as she moved toward
Sheriff Wright.

He looked at her, his blue eyes brittle and hollow. She so
rarely viewed those eyes—downcast as they often were or
hidden in the shadow of his hat brim. "No."

"But it is true." Mason Wright was the kind of man who
would take Arlington's loss as a personal failure, ignoring
all the lives—including hers—he had just saved, and she
hated that. Hated that she'd fail in this attempt just as she
failed in *every* attempt to make him see his worth.

He held her gaze just then. "No," he repeated, but only a
little softer. Then his attention spread out beyond her to take
in the larger crisis at hand.

"Is she the other agent?" He nodded toward Rebecca
Sterling and the upset children, now surrounded by the few
other railcar passengers. "Liam mentioned a Miss..."

"Sterling, yes, that's her. Liam!" Holly suddenly remembered the brave orphan boy who'd run off to get help. "Is
Liam all right?"

"Shaken, but fine. Clever boy."

"I was so worried, sending him off."

He looked at her again, this time with something she could almost fool herself into thinking was admiration. "It was quick and clever. If anyone saved the day here, it was you."

Holly blinked. From Mason Wright, that was akin to a complimentary gush. "It was the only thing I could think of to do."

A child's cry turned them both toward the bedlam surrounding Miss Sterling. The children were understandably out of control with fear and shock, and Miss Sterling didn't seem to be in any shape to take things in hand. Who would be in such a situation?

She would, that's who. Holly was an excellent teacher with a full bag of tricks at her disposal to wrangle unruly children. With one more deep breath, she strode off to save the day a second time.

Don't miss FAMILY LESSONS
by Allie Pleiter, available April 2013
from Love Inspired Historical.